REBEL

REBEL

HER PARANORMAL MAJESTY'S SECRET SERVICE™
BOOK 03

MICHAEL ANDERLE

THE REBEL TEAM

Thanks to the Beta Readers
James Caplan, Larry Omans, John Ashmore, Kelly O'Donnell,
Mary Morris

Thanks to the JIT Readers
Dave Hicks
Deb Mader
Debi Sateren
Dorothy Lloyd
Jackey Hankard-Brodie
Jeff Eaton
Jeff Goode
Larry Omans
Lori Hendricks
Micky Cocker
Paul Westman
Peter Manis

If I've missed anyone, please let me know!

Editor
The Skyhunter Editing Team

LMBPN Publishing
PMB 196, 2540 South Maryland Pkwy
Las Vegas, NV 89109

First US Edition, December 2020
(Previously published as a part of *Rogue, Renegade & Rebel*)
Version 1.01, February 2021
ebook ISBN: 978-1-64971-396-4
Print ISBN: 978-1-64971-397-1

DEDICATION

*To Family, Friends and
Those Who Love
to Read.
May We All Enjoy Grace
to Live the Life We Are
Called.*

— Michael

GENEVIEVE KING'S
UK TO US TRAVEL GUIDE

An insight into how the Americans butcher the queen's English

UK (Correct) — *US (Wrong)*

- **Aluminium (*ah-luh-min-ee-um*)** — Aluminum (*ah-loo-min-uhm…*WHAT?)
- **American Football** — *Football*
- **Bathroom / Toilet / Loo** — *Restroom*
- **Biscuit** — *Cookie*
- **Bonnet (Car)** — *Hood*
- **Broadsheet** — *Newspaper*
- **Car Park** — *Parking Lot*
- **Chips** — *French Fries*
- **Crisps** — *Potato Chips*
- **Dual carriageway** — *Highway, freeway*
- **Dummy** — *Pacifier*
- **Duvet** — *Blanket (yes there are duvets, but not in this story)*
- **Extension lead** — *Extension cord*
- **Flat** — *Apartment*
- **Football** — *Soccer*
- **Garden** — *Yard*
- **Holiday** — *Vacation*
- **Ice lolly** — *Popsicle*
- **Jumper** — *Sweater*
- **Knickers** — *Panties*
- **Lift** — *Elevator*
- **Lorry** — *Truck*
- **Mad** — *Insane / Crazy*
- **Motorway** — *Highway*
- **Mummy** — *Mommy*

- **Nappy** — *Diaper*
- **Number Plate** — *License Plate*
- **Oregano (*or-i-gah-no*)** — *Oregano (or-eh-ga-no...I mean, come on!)*
- **Pants** — *Underwear*
- **Pavement** — *Sidewalk*
- **Peckish** — *Hungry*
- **Police / Bobbies / Pigs / Boys in Blue** — *Cops / Police*
- **Potato (*poh-tah-to*)** — *Potato (pah-tay-to)*
- **Rubbish** — *Trash*
- **Shop** — *Store*
- **Sofa** — *Couch*
- **Sweets** — *Candy*
- **Torch** — *Flashlight*
- **Tomato (*toh-mah-to*)** — *Tomato (tah-may-to)*
- **Trainers** — *Sneakers*
- **Trollied** — *Drunk/plastered*
- **Trousers** — *Pants*
- **Tube** — *Subway*
- **Waistcoat** — *Vest*
- **Wardrobe** — *Closet*
- **Windscreen** — *Windshield*

PROLOGUE

<u>Midtown Manhattan, New York City</u>

Something strange had gone down in New York City yesterday. Police now patrolled the streets in force, and Times Square was cordoned off for examination by the federal authorities.

Kate Gallagher had spent an hour or so roaming around the square so far that morning. Unable to be seen by any of the boys in blue, she had examined the area to get some indication of what had gone on.

"It came out of nowhere," an eyewitness told a cop with a notepad from the back of his car. "It was a regular night. We were on our way home from a showing of *Kinky Boots*. The next thing we knew, it was impossible to see anything."

A fog cloud had masked the living from being able to see anything. It seemed like the perfect cover-up for something...otherworldly.

Kate eavesdropped on more conversations as she bypassed the cops to get to the people in lab coats who were gathering evidence from the spot the cloud had originated from. Scattered, broken glass confirmed eyewitness accounts of something being thrown to activate the fog, but the compound was untraceable. There were no samples to take.

"Impossible," one forensic psychologist exclaimed.

"Never in my life…" said another.

Only one man had seemed to have any inkling of what might have transpired in the square.

Kate had spotted him earlier, flashing a badge and strolling around like he owned the place. A guy who could not have looked more like a federal agent if he tried.

His black suit was pristine. He wore dark aviator shades and an earpiece that coiled down into the inside of his jacket. His immaculate shoes reflected the lights on their surface.

The man touched a finger to his ear and spoke so quietly the others could not hear a word he said. Kate heard him clearly. Standing so close to the man, it would have been impossible *not* to hear.

Whispers of "specters" and contacting "Her Majesty" and "impossible this could have flown under our radar," were made.

Kate gave a derisive snort over his shoulder. The man's hand unconsciously brushed away the puff of air, and then she was gone from the Square.

There would be no more information she could get from the mortals.

Tracing the specters would be the difficult part. Since whatever showdown had occurred, the entire city appeared to be in hiding. Normally, Kate could walk down any street in London and bump into four specters before she'd hit the first corner. But here…

Gordon Owens, a specter with a square jaw and a body that looked like it was crafted by the gods, met her on the corner of Sixth and Thirty-Eighth. "Anything?"

Kate shook her head. "Just a load of mortal mumbo-jumbo. The Beaters have finally shown their faces, but I think it'll be some time before they determine the truth of what transpired."

Gordon's jaw tightened. He wasn't a fan of Beaters. The US Government's Spectral Service was a relatively new department, but that didn't prevent the agents from interfering. Like all of the letters agencies, the people who worked for them believed they were the top dogs in the equation—and now they were involving themselves in this. "Without a spectral unit to guide them, they're not going to get much more information than we have. There has to be someone around here we can pull the information from."

Kate nodded her agreement, and they started looking for a witness the mortals couldn't get to first.

They hunted all over Times Square, exploring nearby alleyways, searching in the subway stations, and even stalking several of the high-rise apartment blocks nearby. They eventually found what they were looking for in the shadow of the Empire State Building.

The specter was howling in the middle of the road. Had she been mortal, she would have been either carted off to the hospital or arrested for public nuisance and removed.

As it was, the cars drove straight through her without consideration.

Kate smiled. She was exactly the type of specter they were looking for. She nodded at the woman and bent to get a grip under her arms. "Let's get you out of the road."

Gordon chuckled as he lifted the woman's legs. "Easy there," he cautioned when she wailed in his ear.

The woman with the bloated face paused before erupting into even louder high-pitched wails of pain. "You don't understand; it flares up like this sometimes, particularly after a fall."

They carried the woman out of the street, ignoring her cries of "careful," and "I don't bend that way!" until they were in a quiet space where they cross-examined the witness and tried to deduce what she knew.

The woman told them as much as she could remember.

Although the event had transpired only twenty-four hours ago, she insisted her memory was foggy from the pain.

Kate and Gordon did their best to remain patient throughout her recounting of the tale, and soon they had enough information to be moving along with.

The woman was outraged when they said goodbye. "You're just going to leave me here?"

Gordon gave a patronizing grin. "I'm sure a good nap will cure you of all your ailments."

The woman scoffed as they walked away. "What do you know about pain?"

The specters didn't speak again until they were standing outside of the entrance to the Empire State Building.

Kate glanced up at the building, her position giving her the perception of a never-ending monolith piercing the sky.

There were no yellow and black cordons or flashing blue lights around *this* building.

Kate and Gordon slipped inside easily enough. They climbed the stairs to the top level and came out in the wide, open space which, unknown to the pair, Jennie had exited the day previous.

The lights were off, but they could see well enough to know where they were going.

Kate's skin tingled at the afterglow of spectral energy still lingering around the room. She followed the energy and passed through a door into a smaller room with a view over the entire city.

"Something happened here," she murmured. "Something big."

"You're telling me." Gordon reached down and picked up the ghostly bearskin hat, its black fur so dark it had almost dissolved into the shadows.

Kate's jaw clenched. "Is that... Is he..."

"I don't know of any other dopey-hatted beefeaters in the US," Gordon replied with grim neutrality. "But what happened to him?"

"Isn't it obvious?" a new voice asked.

Kate and Gordon turned in the direction of the door, where a specter in a pinstripe suit leered out from the canopy of his brow. His shoulders were slumped, his entire demeanor one of defeat.

"Who are *you*?" Kate asked.

"The name's Rico," the specter replied glumly. "You won't find anything here. They're all gone. Scattered." He shook his head solemnly. "I've never seen anything like it…"

Kate and Gordon looked at each other, then back at the specter. "You saw what happened here last night?"

"Every damned second of it," Rico replied.

A sly grin crept onto Kate's face. "Please, tell us everything."

CHAPTER ONE

Greater London, England

Jennie hadn't realized how much she'd truly missed her home until the plane had started its descent over the English countryside.

She grabbed her only bag and practically sprinted through the terminal corridors after disembarking, ignoring the crowded moving walkways in favor of the open spaces on either side. She emerged into the overcast British day, taking a deep breath of the chilly air as she rattled her car keys in her pocket, eager to get back to normality.

Her trip to New York had been the longest she'd ever left her baby in the hands of strangers, and now she wanted to check that she had been taken care of.

A quick inspection at the airport parking facility assured her that the extra £1k she had slapped into the attendee's hand had ensured her red Shelby GT500 had been given the VIP treatment.

There wasn't a speck of dust, a scratch, nor so much as a slight build-up of condensation.

"Great work," Jennie enthused, giving the valet a pat on the cheek. She felt his eyes on her ass as she climbed in. She smirked and revved the engine, setting the car in motion.

Jennie tightened her grip on the steering wheel and let the kitty roar.

It felt right being back on the left-hand side of the road. She raced down the M4, the car eating up the dual carriageway as she opened the throttle and gave the car some gas. It responded to her every touch, her intuitive control of the car coming from familiarity. She cut around lorries and sped past the single-file lane of traffic built up on the inside, working its way slowly toward the landscape of London approaching from the distance.

"Jennie!" Baxter shouted, his face growing as red as a specter's could. "*Jennie!*"

Jennie tapped "Mute" on her steering wheel and glared at him. Steppenwolf's *Born to Be Wild* cut out mid-chorus and left Carolyn, Feng-Mian, Lupe, and Baxter in uncomfortable silence.

"I'm sorry," Baxter apologized, the spectral giant struggling to shrink into his seat. "But does the music really have to be that loud? I know you're excited, but eardrums are fragile things, even in the afterlife."

Carolyn leaned forward between the seats. "Can specters' eardrums get damaged by loud noise, then?"

Baxter looked at her like she was a cylinder short of a V8.

Jennie laughed. "You still have a hell of a lot to learn about the ways of living the spectral life." The rules changed a lot once you were dead, but Jennie had lived around the dead and the living long enough to know that what Baxter was saying was absolute bullshit.

She tossed her phone to Baxter. "If you don't like my music, why don't *you* put something on?"

He fumbled as he caught the phone, spent a few minutes scrolling through her playlists, then gave up and docked the phone in its cradle on the dashboard. "There's nothing there I like."

"Nothing?" Jennie grinned, then swerved back into the outer lane to overtake the snarl of six cars ahead.

"Anyway, it wasn't the music choice," Baxter continued, "it was the volume. Honestly, after having to endure a seven-hour flight with that baby screaming, I thought we'd get a bit of a chance to relax in the car and prepare for what's ahead."

"Oh, Jesus," Carolyn exclaimed. "That baby would *not* shut up. Why didn't the mom do something?"

Lupe scowled. *"Los bebés deben ser prohibidos en los aviones."*

"Lupe!" Jennie exclaimed. "Really?"

"What did he just say?" Carolyn asked.

Jennie pouted. "He wants to ban babies."

"From planes," Lupe clarified. "I forgot you speak Spanish."

"It's not the worst idea." Carolyn turned to Lupe, confused by his sudden switch of language. "How come you've become more Latino since we've landed in England?"

Lupe shrugged. "Closer to my homeland, I guess."

"Your homeland is Mexico," Jennie reminded him.

Lupe ignored the comment and looked out of the window, watching the rolling hills turn to concrete estates.

Feng Mian remained silent, eyes closed as if in deep thought.

"The point is," Baxter cut in, swinging the direction of the conversation back to their objective. "We've got to have some kind of plan, right? We're not literally going to be running straight into the heart of Buckingham Palace so we can confront the queen, are we?"

Jennie looked over the top of her glasses at him.

"You're kidding?" Baxter shook his head, flummoxed.

Jennie raised her glasses and laughed. "Come on, do you really think I'd be stupid enough to go head-to-head with the queen like that? Who do you think has more understanding of the inner workings of her kingdom than anyone here?" She pointed a thumb at herself. "Trust me, I've got a plan."

Baxter looked at her expectantly.

"What?" Jennie snapped.

"Let's hear your plan," Carolyn urged.

Jennie sighed. "There's really no mystery left in the world, is there?" She tapped a number into her phone, and a moment later, the car was filled with the dial tone.

Several rings later, the phone went to voicemail.

Silence filled the car.

"They're not very responsive," Carolyn commented unhelpfully.

Jennie eyed Carolyn in the rearview mirror. "They're clearly busy."

Carolyn held up her hands. "Okay."

"I can try them again later." Jennie pressed her foot down on the accelerator and slid into the outside lane, overtaking a truck and a couple of family cars.

"So, where are you taking us now?" Carolyn asked, seeing a sign for London City Center streak past.

"Someplace safe," Jennie told her.

"Is there really such a thing in London?" Baxter asked. "Won't the queen have all her specters keeping an eye out for us?"

Jennie smirked. "You don't work in this business for as long as I have without learning a few of the secrets the city has to offer. Trust me. It'll be a piece of cake."

Carolyn and Lupe exchanged nervous glances but remained silent.

Piccadilly Circus, London

George Wheatcroft had been a diplomat in life. He had spent his life negotiating deals. He had sat on the bench in the House of Commons and argued with the Prime Ministers of Great Britain until he was blue in the face.

Well, that part had been fun...

Talking had been his life. Guided by his staunch moral

compass, his policies and viewpoints were often controversial, but at least they were consistent. If there was one thing George could never be called, it was "two-faced."

George always wore his heart on his sleeve, and eventually, at the prime age of forty-two, he had resigned from the party when the majority had voted in favor of a policy he could not stand behind.

Three weeks later, the stress of fighting a losing battle took its toll on his heart.

When he had come back as a specter, he had been given the chance to swear to the crown and join the paranormal court. Disoriented and drawn to the familiarity of order, he had taken the oath immediately, believing that if he couldn't do the good he wanted to in life, he could make an impact in death.

Little did he know just how far from the truth that would be.

George stood in the square and nodded in agreement with the other specters gathered around Shaftesbury memorial fountain. Atop the ornate stone fountain, a winged figure loomed with his bow and arrow, aiming at the people passing in the street.

The specters were out in daylight, but there was no way the mortals could see them.

George looked at the mortals passing naively by with concern gnawing at him. *Why do I feel so nervous?*

Beside him, children threw pennies into the water, giggling as they closed their eyes and made their wishes. Their innocence contrasted against the subject matter being spewed from Kershaw's mouth.

"The enemy is coming," Kershaw growled, his face a sour twist. "Make no mistake, this may be the greatest challenge we've faced in years."

"She's just one woman," a specter to Kershaw's right scoffed, pulling at the collar of her duffel coat, which bunched up around her neck. "One woman against hundreds of specters. What's the worst she can do?"

George was often reminded of a tortoise when he saw Melissa Richmond.

Kershaw glared at Melissa. "You've heard of what Rogue's capable of. You know what she can do."

Melissa shook her head. As the youngest specter among them, she had heard the rumors, but that didn't mean she'd believe them without any evidence to confirm the tales.

"It's bullshit." Melissa scowled. "I've encountered people like her in life. Their reputation precedes them, and it's usually a letdown when you meet them for real. Half of a magician's tricks depend on people *believing* in what they're doing. They're not actually performing magic, it's all just fakery."

Darren Lockey, the specter standing beside George, scoffed. "You're calling Rogue's abilities fake?"

Melissa nodded and crossed her arms. "Damn right. I'm saying it's all bullshit. That the queen uses her to strike fear into the hearts of our enemies. She's mortal. Normal people do normal deeds, but history is written by the victors."

Darren clenched his fists. He had died in a blood-stained hospital gown, and now that was all he would wear for the rest of his existence. Surgery gone wrong was not the best way to induct himself into the land of the dead, especially not at the age of thirty-three.

"You haven't seen what I've seen." Darren scowled, advancing toward the fountain. His body slipped through the stone, and he walked slowly as he spoke. "If you'd been anywhere near her, you'd know she's no mortal human."

A flicker of doubt betrayed Melissa's position. "And you're going to say you have?"

Darren nodded. "You're damn right. In 1982, a patient escaped Broadmoor Psychiatric Hospital with nothing on him but a knife. He finds his way to the local village and frightened the congregation in the church. They terrified him with their reaction to his nakedness and the knife."

"What happened?" Melissa asked.

Locked up for twenty-two years and finally around normal humans?" Darren shook his head. "He went on a killing spree. Blood painted the pews. He turned the knife on himself. The local news called it the worst mass homicide of the decade. But they had no idea of what was to come."

The other specters waited patiently. Many of them had heard the tale in some form or another.

Kershaw gritted his teeth and remained silent while Melissa was enraptured.

"What happened?" she urged.

Darren obliged. "Three weeks later, after the majority of the blood had been cleaned, the church reopened for Sunday service. Reverend Pascal led the service for the anxious church-goers. But when the church bells tolled midday, and the Reverend let out a relieved smile at the end of the service, the poltergeists came."

Melissa gulped.

Darren's voice was hypnotic as he wove a picture of the events in the church. "The unrestful specters of the murdered worshippers flew around the church and whipped up a storm. The doors locked and couldn't be opened by the trapped people. The killer floated around amongst the chaos while the poltergeists threw peoples' belongings across the room, poured melted wax from candles onto the congregation. Some of them were so badly scared that their hair turned white."

Melissa's voice was the barest of whispers. "How did they escape?"

Darren perched on the edge of the fountain closest to Melissa. "Rogue. She materialized inside the church as if she were one of us. I couldn't tell *what* she did exactly, but she drew the poltergeists to her and brought them under her control. The battle wasn't long, and there wasn't a glimpse of fear on her face. Nothing. She came, she saw, she conquered."

His eyes locked onto hers, his dark pupils boring into her.

"She has powers beyond our understanding. Don't underestimate her."

All the specters nodded. They had their own tales to tell, whether of firsthand experience or stories from friends.

Melissa looked down at her feet. "I had no idea."

"Exactly," Kershaw told her gently, reasserting his place as leader of the Piccadilly specters. "No one fears the tiger when it's inside the cage. It's only when she's let loose that the danger becomes real. The spectral world is on full alert. The queen's message is clear. Rogue is coming. It is up to us as specters of the paranormal court to ensure we do everything in our power to stop Rogue in her tracks and guarantee Her Majesty remains secure."

"What brought on the sudden change of allegiance?" Melissa asked Kershaw. When he turned to her, she withered. "I only ask, because…Surely, she's oath-bound to the crown, just like the rest of us? Bound to the queen's Court?"

"Rogue has revealed herself to be a traitor," Kershaw reiterated. "While I don't know the specifics, what I do know is she was recently sent to the US to aid the queen in her endeavors. She aided the enemy instead, and revealed to her personal specter that she had never taken an oath."

There was an audible gasp from the group of specters.

"How is that even possible?" one asked.

"This oversight is severe, yes," Kershaw admitted. "But we are dealing with the consequences."

"So, she truly has gone Rogue," a specter with sleepy eyes and a large sword strapped to his waist muttered.

"Remain vigilant," Kershaw continued as if no one had spoken. "This is not a drill. It is your solemn duty to report any misgivings or suspicious behavior *immediately*. You are to make your way to your assigned lookout position and keep your eyes peeled. We don't know where she'll be coming from. We don't know when she'll get here. What we do know is she *is* coming."

His voice lowered a few notches as he grinned. "Let me be clear: anyone who plays a significant part in protecting the queen will be greatly rewarded by Her Majesty afterward. We work as one. We conquer as one. Got it?"

"Got it," they chorused back.

Kershaw sent them on their separate ways.

George walked to his post in thoughtful silence, his head swimming from this latest revelation. He knew Rogue. He had known her well. Rogue was part of the reason George was still around today and hadn't been exorcised within the first few months of his spectral existence.

George had always been a good judge of character, and he could not have sensed anything within Rogue that made her an enemy of their cause. Rogue fought for justice. Rogue delivered the queen's justice.

Then what the hell was happening now?

George rounded the corner and London's Royal Academy of Arts came into view. It would be just like the drills, which were suddenly a comforting memory rather than the source of deep misery he'd experienced when they were happening.

He'd go up to the roof of this building just like he was expected to, and he'd stand and keep a lookout over the streets for anything out of the ordinary.

Little did he know he would not need to look too far. He climbed onto the roof and opened the lockbox he kept up there. It contained sentimental trinkets and valuables that reminded him of simpler times and kept him connected to his former life.

A flashing LED in the bottom of the box caught his eye. He picked up the ancient Nokia and activated the screen. The screen flickered and displayed a missed call. He viewed the contact and dropped the phone back in the box in shock.

CHAPTER TWO

<u>Piccadilly Circus, England</u>

Knowing the primary spots where the queen's rule reached into the outskirts of London, Jennie drove to a friendly mechanic she knew of on the edge of the city, where she waited until nightfall and made her way into the city via the London Underground.

Perhaps she might have stood out like a sore thumb in the daytime, but dressed in her traveling clothes, she was nothing more than another commuter in a long coat with their hood high to guard their face against the gentle downpour.

"That must have been really hard for you," Baxter empathized, keeping stride with Jennie as she beelined for the tube station.

No one had uttered a word since leaving the car at the garage. Jennie had made it clear in her exchange with the mechanic that she was nervous about what she was asking, but knew it was the right decision in the long run.

"Red is far too noticeable," she muttered. "People already know to look out for her. She needs a new lick of paint. Cloak her like the shadows, and we'll be riding around in the moonlight on the steel wheels of a night-wraith."

Baxter shuddered. Wraiths were something of a legend

among the specters, ancient spirits who inhabited barrows, or old pagan cemeteries in the oldest villages and hamlets dotted around the countryside.

Lupe fell in behind Jennie since his short stature made it difficult for him to keep in step with her. Feng Mian focused on the way ahead while Carolyn looked around with mouth agape. She had always wanted to visit London, and now that she was here, it was everything she thought it would be.

That was especially true when Jennie took a right and they arrived outside a Victorian pub, complete with its original façade.

They ducked inside, and Jennie removed her hood for the first time since they had left the car behind. The dark hood accentuated the color of her hair and brought out the flush of her cheeks. Several patrons turned her way, muttering to their friends as she passed.

Jennie flagged the barkeeper down. "I need room Two for the night."

The barkeeper's eyes roamed down the smooth skin of her neck toward her cleavage.

Jennie cleared her throat and pointed at her eyes. "Up here, slimeball. If you want *that*, I'd expect you to offer a hefty discount."

The barkeeper flushed and stammered over his words. Soon he passed over a key and pointed her up a set of wooden stairs. "Room Four. Second door on your right."

"Is Number Two free?" Jennie asked.

Carolyn scoffed.

Lupe shot her a look. "Oh, grow up."

The barkeeper looked perplexed. "I'm sorry, miss. Room Two is occupied until Thursday. If you want another room, I have Five and Seven available."

Jennie leaned against the counter, increasing the young man's challenge of not allowing his eyes to stray down to her chest again. "I don't believe we've met. You must be new blood, yes?"

The barkeeper nodded his head emphatically. "Started last week. This is my first evening shift."

Jennie smiled. "I thought as much. In that case, you should know your boss and I have an arrangement. He keeps Room Two clear for me when I arrive, so I can spend a night in familiar comfort." She dug into her pocket without taking her eye off him and slid £500 in fifty-pound notes across the bar. "This is for you. Fifty-fifty split with your boss. I ask again, is Number Two available?"

As the barkeeper struggled to think of what to say or do, an elderly gentleman with thick silver eyebrows and a hardened face appeared around the corner. "Joseph, what's going on over—"

He paused when he saw Jennie, making no effort to avoid looking at her chest. "Jennie…What a lovely surprise. The usual room is it?"

Jennie straightened up again. "Yes, thank you, Larry."

The barkeeper straightened his back. "Sir, I was just telling her that someone is already in…"

Larry cut him off with a look. "Nonsense! Jennie is one of our favored customers." He raised a hand apologetically. "Just allow us a few moments to get the room in order, and it's yours."

Larry disappeared upstairs, and soon they could hear the disgruntled complaints of a man and woman above them. Footsteps stamped across the landing, and a few minutes later, a door slammed shut.

Larry came downstairs with a slight limp in his left leg and gave Jennie a broad grin. "Room Two is now available for you and your, er…" He eyed Lupe's hood with a certain level of curiosity. "Friend?"

"I knew I could count on you, Larry." Jennie took the key from his hand and blew him a kiss as she headed upstairs.

"I bet you *loved* that." Carolyn laughed. "Man, did you see that? He went redder than an asphyxiated tomato."

Baxter raised an eyebrow. "Hey, don't judge unless she's pulled that shit on you."

Jennie laughed.

"You know what I mean," Carolyn continued. "And the old guy? Bending over so far backward I thought he'd snap in two. Man, to have that power in mortal life."

The room was quaint and clean, with wood-paneled walls and a thick glass window overlooking the street. Jennie sat on the edge of the bed and rooted through her suitcase. Metal clinked against metal, and Baxter spotted several small black cell phones rattling around the bottom of the case.

Lupe placed his bag down and unzipped the top. He pulled out several wrinkled shirts and started to look around.

"What are you doing?" Jennie asked.

Lupe shook the shirts. "Finding somewhere to hang these. If this is to be our base of operations, I want my clothes on hand."

Carolyn laughed. "You're concerned about your clothes? You look like you're heading for Satan-con most of the time, why the sudden interest?"

Lupe's cheeks reddened. "I've never been to Europe, let alone London. I thought I'd make an effort."

"Save the effort," Baxter told him with a broad grin. "My guess is that wherever we're going, no one will give a shit what you look like."

Lupe's face soured. "Fine."

"Besides…" Jennie pulled out a leather purse from her bag and held up the old-fashioned brass key she retrieved from it. "We're not staying here tonight."

Jennie crossed the room over to where a large tapestry hung from the wall. The image had faded, and frayed threads had torn free. She reached up and grabbed the rail from which the tapestry hung and removed it from the wall to reveal a large area of plain white plaster.

Jennie pressed her ear to the wall and moved along it slowly, tapping with her knuckle until she heard a hollow echo in return. She scratched at the wall until a small notch appeared.

"She's done it," Baxter whispered.

"She has?" Carolyn replied.

"Yep." He shook his head. "She's finally gone mad…"

Jennie ignored the comments. She screwed her eyes shut and took a deep breath, then blew on the notch with gusto. Dust kicked up in clouds, and white chalk sprayed out of the keyhole Jennie's effort revealed on the wall.

Jennie inserted the key, twisted it in the lock, and a metallic *"clink"* indicated the mechanism had moved. "Give me a hand with this, will you?" she asked, leaning her shoulder against the wall to push.

Lupe, Baxter, and Feng Mian all pushed together with Jennie, and the door began to swing inwards. Carolyn leapt to help and disappeared halfway through the wall before remembering she needed to focus on becoming material to aid in their efforts.

When the door was open wide enough to slip through, Jennie stopped pushing and grabbed her suitcase from the bed. She double-checked that she'd locked the main door to her room behind her and slipped through the secret door. She worked with the others to push the door closed, blocking the way back.

Jennie turned, her feet immediately found the familiar stairs leading down through the thin cavities between the old pub's walls. The stairs cut around the building, the passageway narrow enough to mean they had to go single file and walk sideways.

Lupe tentatively followed Jennie, breathing in so he could maneuver his way down.

"Where is she taking us?" Carolyn whispered.

Baxter shrugged, his wide spectral shoulders lost in the walls while the center of his body filled the entire passage.

The stairs led down and down, taking a right turn every once in a while. When the streetlights vanished from the small gaps in the wood and plaster, Jennie switched on a torch and guided them through the darkness.

They followed the torch beam until they were completely underground, where the tunnels widened around them.

Baxter's head scraped the ceiling, which might have been a problem if he had been alive. "Where are we?" he asked, his mouth hanging open in awe of the tunnel systems around him.

"The crawl spaces of London," Jennie told him. "A labyrinth used throughout the years to protect the citizens of London from danger. Long-since abandoned and forgotten."

"But what were they used for?" Carolyn prodded. A scratch in the wall beside her showed rough sketchings of fish shapes, rats, and people with crosses for eyes. One image they passed showed a human-like creature with a bird's beak and a wide-brimmed hat.

"Many things throughout the years, for those who knew they existed," Jennie replied as she counted her way past junctions and turnings. "During the Plague, many people fled down here in an effort to escape the disease. Hundreds upon hundreds of Londoners came this way, all hoping to escape what promised to be their deaths."

Lupe shuddered, the chill of the tunnels working its way under his skin. "How did that work out?"

Baxter stroked his hand against the wall. The farther along they got, the more of the strange crow-like humans they saw etched in faded charcoal. Pits filled with bodies and Xs marked through them. "Not very well, it seems."

Jennie nodded. "The tunnels were always a temporary solution. Some fled here during the Great Fire of London, others ducked under here during the World Wars to escape the bombs, planes, and destruction.

"Over the years they've had their uses, but they've all been blocked or forgotten. The government blocked off the known entrances and condemned the tunnels forever as part of measures to keep control as mass immigration increased."

Something large rumbled in the spaces above them, gone as quickly as it came. Thin sprays of dust filtered from the ceiling.

"And yet we're down here," Baxter complained.

"Relax, that was just an underground train," Jennie told him. "It's not like you're the one who's going to get crushed if the ceiling caves in, is it?"

Lupe's eyes widened, and he increased his pace to keep up with Jennie.

After almost an hour of walking in moderate quiet, Baxter was almost certain Jennie had lost her way.

The paintings and sketches had long-since tapered off, and the tunnels had become nothing more than a never-ending sequence of packed-dirt stretches that led to who-knew-where.

Jennie, however, confidently led the way. Her face was smudged and greased with dirt, and they caught their first whiff of semi-fresh air for some time when she came at last to a tunnel that veered right and began to slope upward.

The packed dirt gave way to a set of stairs that led back toward the surface. The higher they climbed, the more the familiar sounds of city life came back into hearing range.

Jennie came to the top of the stairs and unlocked the large paneled square above their heads with the same key she'd used before. She gave the hatch a shove with her upper back.

The wooden hatch gave way, and a spectral hand reached down to Jennie. She took it and allowed herself to be pulled up.

"Took your time." The specter grinned. "I thought they might've already caught you."

CHAPTER THREE

Covent Garden, London

The room was a contemporary shrine to the past.

Metallic signs decorated the walls, each with the legend, *The Savoy Theatre*. A sparkling chandelier hung from the ceiling. Black leather sofas complimented the clean white marble tiles of the floors. Mirrors skirted with lightbulbs decorated the walls, and somehow there wasn't a speck of dust to be seen.

Jennie grinned, her arms held wide. "Welcome to *mi casa*."

"That means 'my house,'" Lupe whispered to Baxter, who immediately rolled his eyes.

Jennie smirked. "Before anyone says anything. Outside of my good buddy George here, you are among the first-ever specters and mortals to ever visit the hidden kingdom of Rogue."

"The first..." Carolyn gasped, looking around. "What is all of this?"

"A collection of things I've collected over the years," Jennie told her. "Things to remind me of where I come from. Where I'm going. Things that hold sentimental value and I like to keep safe." She placed her case in the corner, then put her hands on her hips and looked around. "As for why, well, that's easy to answer. I'm a high-profile spectral assassin serving the queen's, remember? Secrecy is the name of the game. You learn over the years never to trust anyone or show anyone where you live."

"*Was* serving the queen," Baxter corrected.

Jennie pointed at Baxter. "Exactly."

Carolyn rubbed her eyes and shook her head. "I don't get it…"

"What's not to get?" Jennie asked.

Carolyn folded her arms. "If secrecy is the name of the game, then why are you bringing us into your home?"

Jennie hopped over to a small work surface that topped a mini-fridge. She opened the door and pulled out a bottle filled with thick pink liquid. She unscrewed the lid and drank straight from the bottle.

"Ah, yes." She held it toward them. "Pre-mixed cocktails. I'm a genius. Not quite the charm of fresh-made, but good in a pinch."

"Ew." Carolyn sniffed. "Do you ever…"

Jennie grinned. "Put pickle in cocktails? It depends on what I'm in the mood for."

She drank a few more sips and closed her eyes as the cold liquid filtered into her body. When she was quenched, she screwed the lid back and popped the bottle back in the fridge.

"But to answer your question," she continued before Carolyn could nudge her again. "Isn't it obvious? I'm going to need all of your help to make this happen. In every element of my working life, I've been solo except for a designated spectral babysitter who could barely last a mission with me. We never got along. I work better alone."

"Then what's changed?" Carolyn urged. "Not that I'm complaining, of course, I just need to know where we stand."

Lupe grunted in confirmation.

Jennie sat down in a plush leather armchair and studied the unlikely band of specters and mortals standing near the hatch.

She cocked her head to the side. "Because I've never done anything like this before. In my past missions, I've had the totality of the queen's resources on my side. Now they're working against us. That will mean we need to employ every ounce of trickery, misdirection, and cunning we can muster. I'll need diplomats, I'll need fighters, I'll need people with extraordinary abilities on my side."

Carolyn's lip curled. "And you chose us?"

Baxter shook his head. "No. That's not it. It's because we chose *her*."

Jennie raised an eyebrow.

"Think about it," Baxter continued. "Who else followed Jennie without complaint in the battle at Times Square? Who else stayed and guarded Sandra at the Plaza against the loyalist goons? It's us. We're the loyal ones."

"That's not really what I was going for, you soppy git." Jennie smirked. She slapped the arms of the chair and rose. "But if that's what you needed to hear, then there it is. Now, any more questions?"

Carolyn tentatively raised her hand.

"Yes?"

"Just one thing…" Carolyn pointed at the strange specter. "Who the fuck is that?"

The specter laughed. He straightened his tie, placed one hand behind his back, and offered his other to Carolyn. "George Wheatcroft, at your service."

Carolyn cautiously took his hand and shook it. "He's your butler?"

"He's a friend," Jennie replied.

"More than a friend," George corrected.

Baxter raised both eyebrows.

"Not like that, you piece of filth." Jennie laughed. "I might have saved George's life."

"Might have?" George exclaimed. "You should have seen her. Held and pinned by half a dozen poltergeists, three Catholic priests cornering us and about to perform their exorcism when who should be passing by but this glorious example of a woman."

"A happy accident," Jennie dismissed. "I was sent to help with the exorcism of the poltergeists. I can't help it if I saw an innocent specter being used as a diversionary tactic by evil specters."

"Wait a minute," Baxter interrupted. "What do you mean, you were pinned by poltergeists? How did you not realize they're barbaric lunatics who would do anything to save themselves?"

George waved a hand at himself. "Look at me. Do I look like a Victorian specter?"

"No."

"Georgian?"

"No."

"Tudor?"

"Well, no."

"There it is, then. I died seven years ago, so please excuse me if my introduction to the spectral world was not as conventional and straightforward as yours. I thought I was assisting the queen, and it turned out that was far from what I was able to do at the time."

"Poltergeists are bastards," Feng Mian muttered through barely parted lips.

Carolyn and Lupe turned to him in surprise. He had nothing else to say.

"You're right," Jennie agreed. "Poltergeists are bastards, but do you know what's worse? The corruption embedded in the Winter Court."

George took a deep breath. His hand moved to his stomach and he stumbled backward. "*Excuse* me?" he blurted in alarm. "I would never have thought I'd hear those words coming from anyone's mouth, let alone yours."

Jennie crossed the room and put a hand on George's shoulder.

"My dear friend. We've got a lot to catch up on, and you may not like a lot of what you hear. But, stick with me, and I assure you that you'll be on the winning side."

"Winning side..." George frowned. "But doesn't that mean—"

"Enough talk!" Jennie interjected with a broad smile. "Who wants to see the rest of this place?"

Lupe's eyes grew wide. "You mean there's more?"

Baxter and the others explored Jennie's home while Jennie talked George through everything that had happened in America.

It turned out that the room they had entered the house by was the basement. Baxter passed through bathrooms big enough to play badminton in and a number of pristine bedrooms. There was a room dedicated to games and hobbies, and another that was lined wall to wall with various types of weaponry.

This one he took a long time examining, wondering where on earth Jennie had acquired some of the weapons he saw on display. There were rifles, pistols, shotguns, and even a grenade launcher hanging in the firearms section. There were knives and swords and machetes, and a samurai sword that looked like it might once have belonged to a Japanese lord.

The next room was a stark contrast to the weapons room. When Baxter floated through the walls, he was met with rows and rows of theatrical costumes and props hanging off the metal railings.

"She's definitely a character, isn't she?" Baxter muttered to Carolyn, who was already flicking through the various costumes and marveling at the sequins and glamor.

When Baxter came to Jennie's bedroom, a strange warmth fluttered inside of him. The room was unremarkable. Unlike any of the other rooms he had visited already, this room was nothing more than a typical human's bedroom.

A double bed took up the center of the room, while heavy oak furniture held Jennie's clothes and various other trinkets. A dressing table at the side of the room caught his attention. The mirror was smudged and marked in pen.

Unfazed by his lack of reflection in the mirror, Baxter read the message.

Genevieve.

A gift to aid you in the upkeep of your beauty.

(Not that you need it, Princess)

Tucked into the frame beside the writing was a small, black and white photo of a young girl sitting on the knees of a man with perfectly parted hair and a thick mustache, while the woman beside them with bright eyes and pale curls falling around her shoulders looked at them with love.

Baxter longed to know more about these people, who he presumed to be Jennie's parents. He thought about his own family, still sorely disappointed none of them appeared to have chosen the afterlife once they had passed—at least to his knowledge.

Hearing a shout from Carolyn, Baxter reluctantly left the room and found her still in the dressing room.

"Shut the front door…" Carolyn exclaimed.

Baxter looked around, confused. "It is closed."

She clutched a pink feather boa in her hands. "Is this really Jennifer Holliday's boa from the original *Dreamgirls* performance?"

Baxter leaned in closer to get a look at the little label, signed with a tiny black squiggle. "I don't know. Maybe. Hey, have you noticed something strange about this place?"

Carolyn's eyes widened. "Besides the fact that Jennie's got the most *amazing* stuff here? You know she could make a fortune selling this stuff."

"You suggest that again, I'll re-think my earlier speech." Jennie appeared in the doorway. "Come on. Enough snooping. Time to reconvene."

Baxter grabbed Carolyn's arm and pulled her out of the room.

Jennie led them to a second-floor sitting room with curved sofas centered around a glass coffee table.

George sat reclined on the sofa, his face even paler than it should have been.

"It's a lot to take in, isn't it?" Baxter sympathized.

George looked at Baxter as if he had just noticed him for the first time. "You're telling me. All of this…it's true?"

Everyone in the room nodded.

"Every last word," Jennie promised. "The paranormal court has been filled with corruption, and it's down to us to purge it."

"But… It's impossible," George denied. "There are far too many of them—of *us*!" He clapped a hand to his head. "Rogue, I'm a sworn ally of the paranormal court. I can't, in good conscience, betray the queen. It's against my oath. I *have* to tell someone."

"No, you don't," Jennie told him, her face stern. "Has anyone ever stopped to wonder what specters did before the court was first founded? Has any specter ever stopped and asked the question of 'what if' we never made oaths? It's the fear that keeps you all united. The fear of what'll happen if you go against your word, not the magic of the word itself."

"What are you talking about?" Carolyn asked. "I know I may be younger than the rest of you—in every sense of the term—but I saw an entire square filled with devotees of the crown who looked at us with murderous eyes and aimed to destroy us all."

"But they didn't," Jennie reminded her. "The minute we spoke reason to them and showed them another path, they relented. They weren't under the influence of the queen; they were following the crazed orders of a madman who had lied through his teeth to get them on his side."

"So, what would have happened if the queen had directly ordered them?" Baxter asked.

"I don't know," Jennie admitted. "This is all unproven theory, but I have *got* to wonder what came before. There was a time before the court was founded, and specters roamed free. Who invented the oaths? Who made the current rules within which specters now abide?"

"The monarchy," Lupe muttered.

Jennie nodded. "Exactly."

George looked flabbergasted. Jennie had placed a drink in front of him, but he hadn't taken a single sip—nor could he. He eyed the clock on the wall and rose to his feet, wobbling slightly.

"I have to go back," George told her. "I've already been gone too long. If Kershaw sees I've abandoned my post, he'll report me to Her Majesty."

He made it to the door before Jennie pulled him back with a tendril of power. "George." She sounded gravely determined. "You're a good guy. You know right and wrong. You fought for it in life, didn't you?"

George nodded gently. "Yes. But, Rogue. This is different. Terrible things happen to those…"

"Those who get caught," Jennie finished, her expression steely. "Every specter who gets *caught* betraying the crown faces the ultimate punishment. *You* will not get caught."

George stared at her in silence.

"We need an ally, George," Jennie told him softly. "An insider at court. We can't do this without you."

George considered this. "I've got to go."

With a swift turn, he disappeared through the walls and out of sight.

Carolyn's face was filled with panic. "We can't let him go!

We've just told him everything. What if he tells someone else? He knows where you live!"

Jennie shook her head, her lips thin. "No. No, he won't. Out of every specter in the court I've ever met, there's no one else I'd trust as much as him."

"Why?" Baxter asked. "How can you trust someone so?"

Jennie gave no reply.

CHAPTER FOUR

<u>Covent Garden, London</u>

Baxter looked around the room. It had been bugging them since they'd arrived at Jennie's place, but now he finally had it figured. "I've just noticed what's so strange about this place."

"Great to see you're paying attention," Jennie replied absent-mindedly. The map was unfolded on the table in front of them. Small red pins were dotted in locations around the large printout of London, indicating the places where the queen's hold was the strongest—at least, to Jennie's knowledge.

"I'm sorry," Baxter told her. "But it's really been killing me."

"What is it?" Lupe asked.

Baxter made a circle of the room with his finger. "You don't have any windows in any of your rooms. There's no natural light in the whole place."

"You're right," Carolyn agreed. "Now that you mention it, I can't believe we didn't realize it before. Jennie, where are we?"

"Underground," Jennie informed them. "Underneath the Savoy Theatre."

Carolyn's face fell. "Shut up. So, that really was the feather boa Jennifer Holliday wore in *Dreamgirls?*"

Jennie smiled. "That's right. It's actually an import from the Broadway version of the musical, but *Dreamgirls* has been showing every week in the Savoy for years. It only just recently stopped its run here, so that boa is going to go up in value very quickly." Jennie turned to Feng Mian. "Of course, you already know that, don't you, my friend?"

Feng Mian stared silently back at Jennie.

Lupe leaned over the map, clearly uninterested in theater talk. "Doesn't that make this a bit of a problem?"

His finger traced the map to find the Savoy Theater. He followed the lines of the road until his finger tapped on Buckingham Palace. "That's a little over a mile away. Aren't we a bit close for comfort here?"

"The closer we are to danger, the further we are from harm," Jennie replied dryly.

Lupe's eyebrow arched. "Wasn't that a line from *The Lord of the Rings*?"

"*The Two Towers*, I think," Jennie replied. "You know, I actually met Billy Boyd not long after he took that part. Nervous thing, he was, but he managed to do a fantastic job, don't you think?"

Baxter shook his head and laughed.

"What?" Jennie asked.

"Nothing." Baxter turned his attention to Lupe.

"Seriously, aren't we playing it a little close to home?" Lupe continued. "We exit from this place, and the queen will be straight onto us."

Jennie returned her attention to the map. The layout confused the Americans greatly, considering there seemed to be no real order to the city whatsoever. Where New York was built on a grid, London's layout might as well have been drawn by a child.

Jennie took them all through the hotspots on the map, outlining the methodology the queen had employed for her protection. Over the years, the queen had grown complacent in her protection, having ultimate control over the city and most of Western Europe.

Now, Jennie placed clusters of pins in the hotspots where she knew specters would be on the lookout. She also noted George's information that specters across the city had been alerted, and therefore the main streets would be off-limits.

"That doesn't leave us with too many options," Lupe insisted. The map was now covered in red pins. "We're sitting ducks. The minute we leave this pond, we'll be seen."

"What a beautiful analogy," Jennie told him with fake sincerity. "You could be a poet."

Lupe shot her a sour look. "I *was* a poet, once."

Jennie looked at him in surprise, then shrugged. "I guess even the Phantom of the Opera loved his music."

"What's that supposed to mean?" Lupe snapped.

"So, what's our plan?" Baxter interjected before things got heated. "How are you planning to bypass all of the queen's guards? You've said it yourself; she'll have eyes everywhere. Everyone in the city knows what you look like."

"Actually, that's not entirely true," Jennie replied. "Most of my dealings were with the queen or her advisors directly. There may be a few in the palace who know exactly what I look like, but everyone else will be working off a description. That can be easily remedied."

Carolyn clapped excitedly. "Your costumes?"

Jennie chuckled. "In a manner of speaking. I've got plenty of outfits that should mask my identity, so that's part of it, but it'll only get me so far. I've also got something else in mind."

"What is it?" Lupe asked.

Jennie shook her head. "That's for me to know and you to find out later. We're going to have to split up for a short time, okay?"

"Sounds like a recipe for disaster," Baxter mumbled.

Jennie laughed. "It's always nice when your team has confidence in you, isn't it? This is why I always worked solo. Look, I need to do this, okay? I won't be gone for long. A day or two tops. In the meantime, I need you three to do me a favor."

"And what's that?" Lupe asked skeptically.

"You can be the reconnaissance team," Jennie told him. "No one here knows who you are yet. Scout the streets around the palace and see for yourself where the specters are keeping watch. Keep a low profile and report your findings when I get back. Any firsthand information we can get on the situation will be invaluable."

"What about your friend?" Lupe demanded. "What if he leads the queen's army here and rats us out?"

Jennie's face straightened. "If that *does* happen, we're not going to be here for the next twenty-four hours, and I imagine Queeny won't exactly hang around with capturing me if she does catch wind of our location. This way, we get shit done, we keep ourselves safe, and we protect ourselves and learn whether George is truly on our side."

"I thought you said you trust him?" Carolyn pointed out.

Jennie grinned. "Oh, I do, but you can *never* be too careful. Remember, I trusted the queen for over a hundred years. People let you down."

Lupe scoffed. "That's reassuring."

Jennie clapped her hands and stood up. "Well, if we're all clear on who's doing what, I suppose we better get our arses in gear. We've got a court to unravel."

"One more thing." Baxter rose from his seat. "You said the three of us could do you a favor. There are four of us."

Jennie patted Baxter's arm. "Oh, Bax. Did you really think I'd go on my mission solo? I need you, buddy. Saddle up."

On the highest level of Jennie's house was a small door. Carolyn and the others hadn't noticed it before since its color matched the walls around it, but now Jennie gave the door a nudge and it opened.

Behind the door was a small crawl space that rose up a steep slope and met a wall with a combination lock. This she spun until it clicked, and she backed aside to allow Lupe to crawl through while the others floated through the walls.

"You guys be safe, okay?" Jennie instructed, passing Lupe a cell phone. It was simple and black. A burner phone. "Take this. I've put the number from my own phone in there. It's the only one in there, codename, 'Drina.'"

"Drina?" Lupe asked.

Jennie shook her head. "Long story. Queen Victoria's real name is Alexandrina."

"What?" Carolyn exclaimed.

"No time for that," Jennie urged with a smile. "If you need me, call me. Start the conversation with the phrase, 'Hey baby, just thought I'd check in,' if everything is okay. If something's wrong, open with, 'Hey, guuurl.'"

Lupe gave her an incredulous look. "Are you serious?"

Jennie's face told him she was. "Oh, one more thing. There's a spare key on the inside of the door above the fire alarm lever."

Jennie closed the door behind her and left Lupe to crawl out of the escape door. He coughed on a thin haze of dust around him, eventually clambering out into a small janitorial cupboard.

Something fell on top of Lupe, and he panicked. He kicked the object away and made the metal bucket sing. He stood up sharply, scrambling up the walls, and saw that the object had been nothing more than a broom.

Carolyn giggled. "Way to not draw attention to yourself."

Lupe glared at her, then pressed his ear against the door and listened out for anyone on the other side.

"I think it's clear," he whispered just as Feng Mian floated through the wall and gave a swift nod of his head. "Oh, yeah. Forgot you guys could just check the coast for me."

The theater was empty at that time of day. They snuck through the corridors, and up some stairs that led them out the wings of the majestic space. Carolyn peered around the thick red curtains and was struck by the golden décor and the rows upon rows of red velvet chairs.

"I can see why Jennie has such a fascination with this place," Carolyn breathed. "It's beautiful."

Lupe grunted, clearly not taken with the prestige. They left the stage and walked up the aisle in the center to the stairs at the far end of the theatre.

They hurried through the reception, where Lupe rooted around for the key above the door and unlocked it.

It was early morning. Black cab taxis queued outside the adjacent Savoy Hotel, and the concierge gave Lupe a strange look as he opened the glass doors. He nodded at the concierge. "Random security check," he told him before locking the door and speeding down the street.

London unfolded before them. The sun had barely risen, and the sky was a patchwork of purples and pinks. People passed them with briefcases in hand on their way to work. Cars rumbled past, and cyclists sped down the narrow sides of the roads.

Lupe looked around, feeling suddenly very far from home. "Well, we're outside. Where do we start?"

Carolyn's face lit up. "The London Eye? Ooo, how about the London Dungeons? Big Ben? The Houses of Parliament? The Gherkin?"

"You know we're not here to sight-see?" Lupe reminded her. "We're on a reconnaissance mission. That means we stick to the plan and scout what's going on around us."

"I know," Carolyn replied, unabashed. "That doesn't mean we can't take *slight* detours and see some sights, does it? We need to get a lay of the land, so what's your problem?"

Lupe grumbled. "I don't think that's wise. We have to remain focused. We'll skirt the perimeter of the palace, to begin with. When that's done, well, we'll see."

They took a left and turned onto Carting Lane. As they took their time studying the sights around them, Carolyn let out a squeal and ran ahead to where the buildings parted and the River Thames appeared before them.

Lupe caught up with her and took a deep breath when he saw the Thames. The river was wider than he'd thought. On the left was the Waterloo Bridge, and across the water, they could see the London Eye slowly turning on its axis.

Not too far from that, on their side of the water, they could just make out the needled top of Big Ben.

"Which direction are we meant to be heading?" Carolyn asked excitedly.

Lupe unfolded his copy of the map and sighed. "Right."

Carolyn winked. "Toward the sights?"

Lupe nodded and folded the map away. "I suppose so."

Carolyn squealed again. "You know the London Eye is now sponsored by Coca-Cola? Yeah, it's now officially called the Coca-Cola London Eye."

Lupe scoffed. "That's stupid."

"Hey, it's not like the US is much different when it comes to sponsorships, is it? 'American Airlines Center,' 'Bank of America Stadium,' 'Minute Maid Park.' Need I go on?"

"Where's Minute Maid Park?" Lupe asked incredulously.

"Houston," Carolyn replied.

Lupe's gaze wandered as a boat cruised by on the water. A gull cried overhead.

"Okay, fine," he conceded. "We can see some of the landmarks. But can you please focus on searching for specters who may be on the lookout for Jennie while we do?"

Carolyn nodded vigorously. "Of course. Sorry."

"Right." Lupe gave a curt nod and studied the roads and streets around them. "It's surprisingly quiet at the minute."

Feng Mian tapped his shoulder and nodded toward the roof of the nearby building. In their spectral forms, they almost melted into the sky behind them, but Lupe could make out two specters standing like silent sentinels, their eyes cast down toward the group.

Lupe pulled his eyes away.

"Do you think they suspect anything?" Carolyn asked.

Lupe shook his head and began walking toward the Waterloo Bridge. "Not," he reassured them. "As far as they're concerned, we're just a bunch of tourists visiting London." He paused, then added. "Maybe you two should walk several paces back and stop talking directly to me. We don't want to arouse any more suspicion."

Carolyn and Feng Mian agreed, falling in step several meters behind Lupe.

As he walked, Lupe withdrew his map and marked a small red X in the place where the sentinels stood. He could still feel their eyes on him as they crossed over the bridge and made their way closer to the London Eye.

CHAPTER FIVE

The Lost Tunnels, England

Baxter couldn't understand how Jennie knew where she was going. She wandered past a hundred junctions and turnings and didn't lose an ounce of confidence in her way. Her footsteps echoed, and the dark tried to invade the torchlight.

A couple of times along the way, rumbling came from above. Baxter grew used to this over time, but he didn't grow any further confidence in the integrity of the tunnel when loose dirt fell from above.

After an hour or so, Jennie paused and touched her finger to her chin.

"Lost?" Baxter asked.

Jennie gave a derisive snort. "Please. No, I'm just deciding which way would be best to go."

"That's easy," Baxter answered as he turned between the three paths that forked off from their location. "We could go that way, that way, or that way."

Jennie smirked. "Helpful."

Baxter made a flourishing bow. "I try."

Jennie remained silent a moment longer, deliberating her decision.

"What's the dilemma?" Baxter asked, dropping the clown act.

Jennie pointed left. "Well, this way brings us closer to where we need to be, but the exit point is in the basement floors of a very popular football stadium."

"You guys play NFL here?"

"Not American Football, *football*." Jennie mimed kicking a ball with her foot.

Baxter stared at her blankly.

"Soccer?" Jennie clarified.

Baxter grinned as understanding dawned for him. "Oh! *Soccer*. Why didn't you say so? You guys love soccer, right?"

"No!" Jennie snapped. "We like *football*. The game where you kick a ball with your foot and can't touch it with any other part of your body unless you're the goalkeeper."

Baxter laughed. "You Brits are weird."

"We *invented* football," Jennie informed him hotly. "*Hundreds* of years before you guys stole the name. We can call it what we please."

As much as Baxter knew they were there for a reason, the opportunity to rile Jennie was too good to pass up. "Soccer is easier for me to remember."

"Soccer is a lie," Jennie retorted. "Besides, you guys barely kick the ball in the NFL. You pick it up with your hands, run at each other, and occasionally kick it when you're near the end zone. At least in football, it's all feet."

"I didn't know you had a foot fetish," Baxter quipped.

Jennie grew visibly annoyed. "*Football* is football!"

"Hold on, don't you guys have a thing here a little like the NFL? A game where you pick up a normal-shaped ball and throw it and kick it?"

"It's called *rugby!*" Jennie exclaimed, her voice loud enough to echo around the tunnels.

Baxter snorted and shook his head. "Man, are you guys confused on this side of the pond."

Jennie glared at Baxter and took a steadying breath. "Whatever you want to call it, here are our options. Number one, we open up into a *football* stadium and risk being seen by thousands of Chelsea fans, as well as the crown, given that this is a high-profile area. Or, number two, we come out of the bathrooms in the back of an old pub and have a bit further to walk."

"Wow," Baxter remarked. "So, number two is 'become a reverse number two?'"

Jennie shot him a sour look. "Don't be a child."

Baxter lifted his hands. "I opt for number two."

Jennie rolled her eyes and took the path leading straight ahead.

The silence pressed in on them like an enemy as they walked. Baxter's mind wandered back to the time they had spent together in New York. He had never been this far away from home, and he now felt the strangeness of the city around him.

"I still can't believe how fucked up this all is," he thought aloud. "This time last month, I was happy floating between theaters and checking out the latest sound imports used to project audio across large arena-style halls. Now…"

"Now the paranormal world is fucked. I know." Jennie concentrated on her direction as she spoke and. "You know, I've served the paranormal court for over a hundred years. I've fought poltergeists, Bhoots, wraiths, specters, humans, you name it, but never once did I stop to contemplate that it was in the name of a corrupt system."

"You didn't have any inkling?" Baxter asked. "Nothing ?"

Jennie shook her head. "Not really. The queen's rule is strong in Europe. Those who step out of line *really* step out of line. It's hard to argue with the removal of nuisances who decide to meet their end in a display of destruction and violence. All these years, I've been removing drug cartels, mobsters, the corrupt beings of the spectral world. How could I have seen that the one who sits at the head of the spectral world is the most corrupt of all?"

She stared at Baxter with solemn eyes, waiting for an answer he didn't have.

"I don't know," Baxter replied as they bore left past a series of symbols on the wall depicting a fish and crowds of people sketched in black. "It's always been different in the US. I mean, the paranormal court was seen as the authority, but that was years ago. It seemed like the queen cares more about our European cousins, and so organizations have been trying to create some alternative structure for ages. It just so happened that the Spectral Plane was the first to really make headway."

He lifted a shoulder. "It was inevitable, really—the uprising. It's been obvious for years that the queen was only really interested in what was nearby. All of her efforts to communicate with us had been half-assed and washy."

Jennie turned a corner, then stopped and looked at Baxter. "You know she's got contacts within the US Government, right? She may have grown lax on the spectral side until late, but she's been working with the US Government for over ten years now."

"You don't say," Baxter exclaimed. "In what way?"

Jennie shrugged. "I don't know. It's never been my business to know, so I've let it lie. My focus was always on my mission. No one else's. Let the queen play her politics. As long as I could live in peace and do my thing, I was happy."

Baxter sighed. "Look how that turned out for you."

"Right?" Jennie agreed.

"At least with that new costume, you might stand a chance." Baxter looked Jennie up and down, still unable to believe how different she looked.

After the others had left, Jennie had taken a selection of costume items from her rails and decked herself out in what she defined as "modern" clothing.

This meant ditching both her charity shop finds, and her

leather pants and corset, in favor of some more "comfortable" jeans. Her boots were hidden beneath the legs of the pants, and she now wore a dark wig cut in a classic bob. She still wore glasses, although the frames were now more angular and twenty-first century, and she once again used Baxter's spectral energy to hide the weapons attached to her hips.

"It's a different look, huh?" Jennie grinned. "I'm not sure I like the trousers."

Baxter stared at her blankly.

"*Pants.*"

"Oh!" Baxter replied. "Oh, yeah. You guys call underwear 'pants,' don't you? Surely they're better for you than the leather stuff you wear usually?"

Jennie shook her head emphatically. "You'd think so, but no. Those clothes are what defines me. I don't wear them for fashion, I wear them for utility and pain."

Baxter frowned. "Pain?"

Jennie waved the conversation away. "Another story for another time. Ask Worthington if you need to know now."

Baxter shuddered as he remembered the blinding flash of light that had come from the top floor of the Empire State Building as Worthington was exorcised by Sandra.

Jennie stopped and knocked on the packed earth wall beside her. "Yep. We're here."

Baxter's nose wrinkled as he remembered where they were heading.

Option number two.

Kensington, London

The route back to the surface wasn't as disgusting as Jennie had painted it to be. But it still wasn't nice.

Baxter floated through the wall and checked that the coast was clear.

It was a customary thing. Since they were emerging into the men's restroom, it was only polite for Baxter to ensure that even as a specter, Jennie would not see anything she didn't want to see.

To his pain, the restroom wasn't empty.

Two men sat doing their business in the stalls, and another stood and unleashed his bladder at the urinal.

Baxter waited.

And waited.

Finally, some fifteen minutes later, the men in the stalls finished and left the restroom of the old pub. Baxter floated back through the wall and gave Jennie a thumbs up.

Jennie latched onto Baxter and passed through the wall, remaining immaterial until she was safely outside of the restroom. When the coast was clear, she wandered through the pub, ignored by the breakfast crowd, and blinked into the sunshine outside.

The world was much noisier here. The nearby roads were packed with traffic, and the city was awake. Jennie checked her phone and saw that it was almost ten AM.

"Come on," Jennie urged Baxter. "Let's move fast."

While they were likely safer the farther away from the palace they were, Jennie didn't want to take any chances. She strolled with a determined purpose—which turned out to be perfect for blending in considering the majority of foot traffic around them was impatient Londoners marching through the streets.

Soon enough, they crossed a two-lane road and arrived at the open gates of the old cemetery.

"Wow, fancy!" Baxter marveled. "Even in death, your guys are taken care of."

Jennie walked through the gates, following the gravel road that cut through the center of hundreds upon hundreds of marble headstones. They stood out in shades of white, gray, and black. Flowers decorated many of the gravestones, bringing color to the solemnity.

Baxter slowed to read the headstones, wondering what condition his own would be in. It had been years since he'd visited it, but he was sure it wouldn't look like this.

Jennie continued straight on toward a large, white building in the center of the cemetery. When they reached the building, she skirted the outside and continued walking straight on through the graves.

"You know that's disrespectful?" Baxter complained, wondering where Jennie was heading.

"That's just mortal superstition," Jennie retorted. "Believe me, there's hardly a soul buried in this soil who will be in any way affected by us walking across the grass. Nearly all have either been set free or have moved to the great beyond."

Baxter couldn't help but notice Jennie's subtle emphasis on "nearly."

They left the newer, well-kept part of the cemetery behind. The farther they got from the building, the more overgrown and crumbling the graves became. Headstones were cracked or decorated with ivy, and some were nothing more than broken stumps in the ground.

They wandered through knee-high grass that hadn't been stepped on in years.

Baxter wondered if the line of trees between the modern part and the older section were a deliberate attempt from the groundskeepers to hide the mess. The forgotten realms where no mortal would come to visit their dead again.

The trees closed around them. The grass here was reaching hip-height. Jennie made her way around the crumbled ruins of an old wall and pushed ivy aside to reveal the remnants of an old mausoleum, its roof long-since caved-in.

In the center of the ruins were several long, stone coffins with heavy lids. Baxter was reminded of the vampire movie he had watched over the shoulders of a couple of mortals one Halloween.

"We're here for vampires?"

Jennie shook her head. "Vampires aren't real."

"How do you know?" Baxter countered. "There was a time when I thought ghosts weren't real, yet here I am."

Jennie bent toward the coffin and ran a hand along its top. "Vampirism is nothing more than a myth. Cult following and absurd rumors spread from accounts of people suffering from genuine diseases. Some believed the symptoms of tuberculosis were proof of vampires. People fear what they don't understand, and believed the infected were drinking the blood of the living."

Baxter's face creased in distaste. "Gross."

"Absolutely," Jennie agreed. "Modern medicine has done enough to debunk any real theory that vampires exist. You know it as well as I do, we've made great progress in the twentieth and twenty-first century."

"I suppose," Baxter replied, still unconvinced. "We exist, though. So, surely there's a possibility vampires could, too?"

Jennie didn't answer. Instead, she closed her eyes and placed her palms flat on the coffin. The disturbing part was that the lids were not securely fastened to the container. Each one lay askew, revealing a thin slice of darkness even the sun was unable to penetrate.

"They're close," Jennie muttered.

Baxter looked around. As far as he was aware, they were alone, lost in the tangles of the cemetery. He realized he couldn't hear the street traffic around the cemetery. He hadn't noticed until that moment, but now that he was paying attention to his senses, he couldn't hear birds, or planes, or anything else.

The quiet pressed upon them.

"Who are *they?*" Baxter asked, his hands moving instinctively toward his weapons.

Jennie smiled. "Hopefully, the people who are going to help us."

"Specters?" Baxter inquired.

Jennie gave a half-shrug. "Of a sort." She stood up straight, kept her eyes closed, and spread her arms wide as she sent out a tendril of energy to connect to Baxter.

"Er, what are you doing?" Baxter asked, feeling her pull on his energy.

"Scanning," Jennie replied simply. She turned a circle on the spot, humming as she did so.

A slight chill began to creep around them, which caused even Baxter in spectral form to shiver.

"This way," Jennie called brightly, coming to a stop with her arms still out. She hopped over the coffins, then vaulted over the wall on the far side of the mausoleum and waded into the grass without waiting for Baxter.

After navigating more trees, they came to another mausoleum, this one far better kept than the one they'd left. The building was built on a hexagonal base with a large stone cross at the top of its roof. A dark marble door barred the entrance.

Jennie approached and pushed the door, her muscles taut as she heaved against the heavy stone.

It creaked open, and the smell of ancient air leaked out. Jennie smiled and clapped her hands as she walked inside.

"Wait!" Baxter hesitated as he eyed the stone carvings. "This building is older than the previous one. Why has this fared better against the elements?"

He was right. Compared to the other building, this mausoleum looked unmarked, as though it had specifically been cared for by the groundskeeper, while the other had been left to ruin.

"They protect it," Jennie told him. "Those who are dead and wish to be left that way. Only under the roof of their forebears can they remain forever together."

Baxter gave a small nod, his face curdling. "Then we really are where I think we are?"

"That depends where you think we are." Jennie smiled as if they were simply walking to the shops to grab some candy.

Baxter swallowed. A single word escaped his mouth. "Wraiths."

Jennie leaned out of the doorway, grabbed Baxter's hand, and dragged him inside.

CHAPTER SIX

<u>Westminster, London</u>

Things grew more complicated the closer Carolyn, Lupe, and Feng Mian got to Buckingham Palace.

They did their best to keep an eye out on the city whilst enjoying the sights. Even Lupe got into the spirit when they approached the London Eye and saw the large wheel slowly revolving.

Carolyn begged to go on the ride, but the queue was far too long. Even if Carolyn and Feng Mian boarded the pods, Lupe would have to either queue for several hours or hang around and wait for the half-hour ride to end. Not only that, but they saw several official-looking specters standing by the Eye, as well as others stationed on the roofs around it.

Lupe marked them on his map and after a heated discussion between him and Carolyn that made the mortals gave him a wide berth, they carried on along the riverbank.

Over the course of the afternoon, they saw Big Ben, the Houses of Parliament, Westminster Abbey, and the Victoria Tower Gardens. Carolyn commented several times about how she wished she had a camera to capture the moment and convinced Lupe to take several selfies on his phone, forgetting until afterward that she wouldn't be visible in any of them.

When they reached St James's Park, they felt the atmosphere change. Whereas the specters they had seen around the Eye were mostly enthusiastic tourists, they now spotted an increasing number of specters roaming the park in watchful silence.

Lupe took a seat on a bench that overlooked the lake. He marked several more Xs on his map and was alarmed to see they were a little under a kilometer from the palace.

"The queen really has the place surrounded, doesn't she?" Carolyn whispered as she sat down beside him and tried to look nonchalant.

Feng Mian stood beside the bench and squinted in the sunlight, eyes scanning the faces of the nearby specters. "Are they all definitely hers?"

Lupe wasn't sure how he could tell, but he felt they were. After twenty minutes or so of observing, he noted that several pairs of specters were walking in short laps around sections of the park. Many of them eyed the three of them with suspicion, mumbling to their partners as they walked.

One pair passed directly by them again. By the third pass, Carolyn hackles began to rise. The specters, a man with a length of stubble covering his face and a pair of dark sunglasses, and a woman wearing a cocktail dress and uncomfortably high heels, turned their heads toward them as they passed and gave them a long stare.

"We should go," Lupe murmured. "I don't like this."

"Did you mark them all off?" Feng Main asked.

Lupe nodded, then rose from the bench and walked back toward the river. He felt many pairs of eyes watching them as they left.

As they reached the borders of the park, Lupe took a right past Downing Street, the home of the Prime Minister, then took a left.

Lupe walked briskly with Carolyn and Feng Mian flanking him.

Carolyn risked a glance over her shoulder. "They're following us," she whispered.

"Who?" Lupe moved to turn his head.

"Don't turn," Carolyn hissed. "It'll raise suspicion."

Lupe clenched his jaw. "How do we lose them?"

"We walk faster," Feng Min told them.

After passing through Parliament Square, the river Thames appeared before them. The afternoon was turning late, and there were mortals everywhere as they began to cross Westminster Bridge and slipped into the streams of pedestrians passing in both directions.

Carolyn kept glancing back to check on the pair following them. "Keep moving. We can lose them if they can't see us."

"Genius," Lupe commented.

"Feng Mian, duck your head," Carolyn instructed, hunching to lose herself in the crowd. "Lupe's small enough to hide, but we're like beacons to them."

Feng Mian walked in a slight crouch while they walked through the crowd. Lupe had to weave around the mortals, which slowed their progress. Carolyn risked another quick look when they reached the other side of the bridge.

"They gone?" Lupe asked.

Carolyn relaxed slightly. "Yes. Although I don't know how long for. Come on, let's duck inside somewhere."

Lupe ran across the street toward the entrance of a pub, making a note to mark off several specters standing on the nearby rooftops when they finally had a chance to stop.

"This is insane," Carolyn hissed. "They're absolutely *everywhere.*"

The map was spread on the table before them. There was an

explosion of red Xs covering the areas they had visited that day, the markings only making up a sixth of the area surrounding the palace.

"Good thing they don't know who *we* are, isn't it?" Carolyn added. "Otherwise, we'd really be fucked."

"It's not like they won't already be suspicious," Lupe reminded her. "Conduits aren't common. If they saw us talking, they're going to start to wonder who I am."

Carolyn looked down at the map, looking at the landmarks they had visited. While it was great to finally see the things she had always wanted to see in life, now that the excitement had worn off, she began to feel a little guilty at being too carefree.

"It's okay," Lupe reassured her, sensing her change in mood. "We just need to be a bit more careful, that's all. What we know is that the closer to Buckingham Palace we go, the more specters there are on patrol." He put his head in his hands and sighed. "I don't know how we're going to sneak past everyone. There's no way in hell we're going to get to the queen. She's too well-guarded."

"Oh, come on," Carolyn told him sternly. "If anyone can do it, it's Jennie and us. There has to be a way past them, right?"

Lupe looked up from the canopy of his hands. "We were still at least a kilometer away from the palace when we saw all those specters. Do you really think that inside the palace won't be even more guarded? If that's what it's like outside, then the inside is going to be crammed wall-to-wall with specters."

"Really?" Carolyn sighed.

"Think about it," Lupe continued. "I've only been involved in the spectral world for a few months, and I'd heard of Rogue before she'd even arrived. Her legend is known worldwide, specters quake before her. You really think the queen won't have her best protection inside to stop Jennie from marching in and destroying her?"

Lupe fell quiet as a barman swept by and collected his empty glass. He offered another beer, and Lupe accepted.

Carolyn waited until the man walked away. "Is that what Jennie wants to do? She wants to kill the queen?" she asked in a near-whisper.

Feng Mian slowly shook his head and spoke. "Jennie does not have murder in her heart. She does not allow her emotions to conflict with justice. She will find the truth and act accordingly. The spectral world will not thank and bow easily to a murderer."

Carolyn laughed. "Then they're going to *love* hearing about what Worthington has been up to on the queen's behalf in the last week."

"He's right," Lupe told Carolyn. He waited for the barman to place his beer down and leave before continuing. "If she kills the queen, who's left to take control of the Crown? There'll be anarchy in the spectral kingdom. Riots. War. It's too great a risk to disrupt the only anchor holding everything together."

"But what about America?" Carolyn asked. "Jennie had no qualms disrupting the status quo there."

"It's different here," a voice behind them answered. "Things are a lot more ingrained in our history."

Lupe almost knocked the table over as he jumped to his feet.

Two spectral heads poked through the wall, a hanging set of stag antlers between them.

Carolyn glared at the pair, instantly recognizing them as the specters who had walked by them at St James's Park.

The specter in the cocktail dress grinned. "You were *not* easy to track down."

Piccadilly Circus, London

George was uneasy as he stood on the roof of the Royal Academy of Arts and watched the people walking beneath him.

He had managed to make it back to his station before anyone

noticed he was missing. While Kershaw could be intimidating at the best of times, he was trusting of his men. That made this part a lot easier.

George's thoughts swirled with conflict about everything Rogue had told him. He had gone through various stages of belief and disbelief, and now he wasn't sure where he stood on the whole ordeal.

She wouldn't lie. She's never once lied to me.

But did he know that for certain? Could Rogue have been lying all along?

No. Of course not. I've lived my entire life around people who lie professionally, and even they have their tells. One way or another, a liar could be sniffed out, and Rogue had only ever been kind and honest with George.

Not that that helped to resolve the conflict. His knowledge bore down on his chest like a bout of severe indigestion. He hadn't experienced the discomfort of an unsettled digestive tract since his death and hadn't missed the sensation one bit. If what Rogue had told him was true, then he had chosen the wrong side. Had dived in at the deep end in death and was trapped.

Or was he?

That had caught his attention—a potential truth that could unravel the very existence of the paranormal court and everything it stood for. If Rogue was right, and oaths were nothing more than a method to control the masses, then perhaps there was a chance that he wouldn't be tied to the darkness forever.

How could George test the theory, though? That was the real question.

Fortunately, the question was tested that afternoon.

Kershaw's head appeared through the floor in a glimmer of spectral blue, unnoticed by George, whose mind was a million miles away.

Kershaw's Neanderthal frown was accompanied by the rest of his body a moment later. He climbed onto the roof without a word and walked over to George, catching him off-guard. "Anything?"

George felt the truth rise in his throat. He saw Rogue in his mind and found himself wanting to tell Kershaw. It hadn't been a problem that he knew where Rogue lived before, given that she existed on the right side of the law. Now he was a weak link, one of the only specters in all of London who knew exactly where she lived and where she had been.

If he told Kershaw, what would happen, then? Would the court send specters to her house to ambush her? Would they wait in silence and pounce on her when she arrived, attacking her by the hundreds?

What would happen to George? Would he be rewarded for his assistance? Would he be reprimanded for not willingly handing over his knowledge after the call for her arrest had been put out? For every second which passed that he didn't tell, was he sacrificing his own future? Increasing the odds of his own eventual exorcism as a withholder of the truth?

Rogue had been good to him. She had been kind. She had saved his life. She asked only this one favor, and he wasn't sure he could keep it.

The lump in his throat rose. He fought the compulsion to say the words he could feel forcing their way out of him. *Yes, Kershaw. I know exactly where she is. Follow me to the Savoy Theater, and I'll show you her hidden underground bunker. She's currently off scoping the guards around the palace and working out her way in to capture the queen, so you might want to hurry. Oh, by the way, I've also got a direct line to her mobile phone.*

He had to. He was a devotee. The oath bound him to the queen. He was sure the words would come, were already tumbling out of him as his mind fought with itself.

He heard himself speak, and his blood ran cold as he caught the words on a dry tongue. "Nope. Nothing yet, Kershaw."

George looked Kershaw in the eye, almost certain he knew it

was all a lie. If George had been human, he'd be sweating right now.

Kershaw held his gaze a moment longer as if trying to read his mind. Finally, he nodded and turned away from the view. "Keep your eyes peeled. Remember, if we're the first ones to spot her, we'll reap the greatest rewards. Keep it up, George."

With that, Kershaw was gone.

George gave a relieved chuckle as he looked over the edge of the roof at the ground below and watched Kershaw track across the street.

What do you know? Maybe Rogue was right, after all.

CHAPTER SEVEN

<u>Kensington, London</u>

The darkness closed in around them. Guided only by Jennie's torch, they worked their way down a spiral staircase and into the depths of the mausoleum.

The stench of age was thick. Cobwebs clung to the ceiling, and somewhere far ahead, something was shuffling around.

"What is that?" Baxter whispered, flinching when his voice was carried far by the echo of the chambers.

"Probably just a rat," Jennie replied in a whisper. "There'll be a few of them here, get used to it."

"I'm used to rats," Baxter replied. "I lived in NYC, remember? It's the other things that put my back up."

Jennie chuckled, and Baxter couldn't see what was so funny. The chill grew the farther down they went, and Jennie didn't so much as shiver.

"Just stay close," Jennie instructed. "You'll be okay as long as you're with me, and don't make any sudden movements."

Baxter shuddered as they reached the bottom of the staircase. "Yeah, because I'm going to be *so* controlled around wraiths. What are we even doing here, Jennie?"

"Acquiring a very necessary ingredient to help us storm the palace." Jennie shone her torch slowly in all directions, revealing a series of rooms with open doors. The walls were lined with the final resting places of the dead, and several skeletons slept forever.

"All of this for some kind of potion?" Baxter hissed.

Jennie put a finger to her lips. "Not exactly. Now shut up, unless you want to upset them."

Baxter's jaw clenched. Wraiths had something of a bad reputation among the dead. The mausoleums that contained the families of the deceased were nothing more than lockboxes to shield the dead from outside influence. A way to ensure the ways of the old world remained untouched.

In the past, family lines were often buried in the same plot, meaning those who were bonded by blood would be taken down into the crypts and given back to their forebears. The isolation and mystery of the wraiths caused a big stir among the modern specters, who couldn't understand the ways of old.

Too many horror stories had been told about the appearance of wraiths in graveyards. Too many Halloween tales of the dead appearing in robes like thick and black smoke, and snatching life from those whom they were envious of the most.

Jennie walked through the crypt, searching for something which Baxter couldn't see. As she shone her torch over the various coffins, things began to shuffle in the darkness behind them.

Several times they heard something akin to the breath of the wind. Once, they heard the ruffling of a cloak being swept away. Whispers began to follow them, but it didn't matter how quickly Baxter turned. He saw nothing, yet he was convinced they were not alone.

They reached a room that was considerably larger than the others. Jennie strode across it and stood before a large, upright coffin. It was easily taller than Baxter, and on the front were carvings in a script made of runes.

Jennie read the text aloud. "Here rests Canute. Brave, loyal, courageous, strong. Spread ye wings and fly."

There was a large pair of angel wings carved into the wall on either side of the coffin. As with many of the other coffins, the front was askew, and a thin line of darkness edged its front.

"How old is this place?" Baxter asked.

Jennie ran a hand along the lid of the coffin and removed some of the dust and dirt which covered the dates. "1016–1035. A millennium."

"Wow," Baxter breathed.

As Jennie rubbed some more dirt from the front of the lid, a strong gust of chill wind ran through the crypt. The sound of the wind passing through the tunnels was haunting. Jennie spun on her heels, the Big Bitch in her hand, aimed at the doorway behind them.

Baxter held his wrench high in one hand and his pistol in the other. His face drained of blood, for standing in the doorway was a creature that appeared to be made of smoke. The smoke coalesced into the shape of a tall, thin creature in a long cloak of black.

If the creature had eyes, there were no signs of them beneath the inky black pit of his hood.

"I was wondering how long it would take you to show your face," Jennie told the wraith softly.

The wraith stared back at them both in silence, the coils of its shadows shifting beneath the hem of the cloak as it hovered several inches off the floor.

The wraith pointed a finger past Jennie, at the coffin behind her. It swept past them and vanished through the coffin.

Jennie turned to Baxter. "Come on."

Baxter frowned. "What, where?"

Jennie pointed at the coffin. "He's taking us to the others."

Baxter stared at Jennie. "The *others*?"

"They're what we're here for." Jennie latched onto Baxter and turned spectral, then made her way through the coffin.

They passed through momentary darkness, coming out on the other side of the wall into a long chamber lined with several candles lit in a spectral green color, where the wraith waited for them.

The wraith turned and floated across the chamber. Jennie could feel the others floating around them as they followed the wraith. Gusts of wind swirled around the place, whipping Jennie's hair about her as she narrowed her eyes and focused on the path ahead.

They entered the chamber, which was lined with the forms of more wraiths. Their arrival sparked a movement in the wraiths, each taking their positions in the chamber as Jennie and Baxter were led to the center by their guide.

Jennie smirked. *Finally.* "Let's parley, shall we?"

Westminster, London

The specter with the dark sunglasses emerged fully into the room and sat in the place Lupe had abandoned. "You're one of them, aren't you?"

"One of what?" Lupe replied, aware of the stares of the other patrons. He lowered his voice, glaring at the specter while he grabbed a chair. "Who are you?"

Carolyn and Feng Mian simply stared at the intruders.

The woman in the cocktail dress joined sunglasses in the booth.

"Apologies for the rude interruption," sunglasses told them with sincerity. "I'm Karl, and this is—"

"Mona," the woman cut in. "Enchanté."

"That's French for, 'Nice to meet you,'" Carolyn remarked with a smug grin.

"You're a conduit, aren't you?" Karl pressed Lupe. "A mortal who can see us and speak to us."

Lupe reached across the table and brought his drink closer, protecting it as though Karl might at any second pick it up and drink it himself. "Who wants to know?"

"Spanish, too," Mona simpered, fanning herself. "What a heartthrob."

Lupe raised an eyebrow. He couldn't remember the last time anyone had called him anything of the kind.

"I'm not Spanish," he muttered, trying not to move his lips too much like some weird form of ventriloquy. His looks already gathered too much attention, what would the public think on seeing him talking to himself in the corner?

"Portuguese?" Karl suggested.

"Does it matter where he's from?" Carolyn snapped. "Why don't you tell us why you've been following us?"

"American," Mona exclaimed. "Interesting. You know, we've heard reports of things kicking off over in America. Some very interesting things, indeed. Rumors of a rebellion. Of war between those who follow the queen's rule, and those who choose to shun it."

"Really?" Carolyn feigned surprise, leaning back in her chair. "That is interesting."

Karl eyed her suspiciously. "That's right. Rumor has it Rogue has returned to the UK and is currently running loose in the city. According to our sources, she's switched sides. You wouldn't know anything about that, would you? You being from the US, and all?"

Carolyn made a show of thinking hard. She chewed her lip and muttered incoherently. "Nothing comes to mind. I actually came to the UK last year on a trip and never left. Haven't heard from my American cousins in months."

"Oh, really?" Karl croaked.

Carolyn nodded, her eyes wide. "Really."

"What are you insinuating?" Lupe demanding, his face growing warm as he felt the pair's scanning eyes. "Are you suggesting a trio of nobodies like us have done something incriminating?"

"Not," Mona assured him. She looked longingly at Lupe's glass. "I miss the taste of beer."

Lupe nudged the cup toward her. "Help yourself."

Mona glared at Lupe. "That's just cruel."

They all sat in silence, staring at each other for a few moments. Somewhere in the bar, someone dropped a glass and a wave of patrons cheered.

"You see, my problem with all of this is that you're all terrible liars." Karl leaned forward and stared at Lupe. "Do you know how I know that?"

Lupe held his stare and remained silent. If things were about to go sour, he had nothing more than a new-born girl and an ancient Chinese specter to fight the pair.

"Every specter has some kind of ability. Did you know that?" Karl scoffed. "Of course, you do. You've been in this game a while, haven't you?"

He waited for Lupe to speak. Lupe didn't oblige.

Karl shrugged. "Okay, then, stay quiet. Do you know how rigid the queen's current protection schedule is? Tight. Tighter than a nun's... Well, you can imagine. This means there aren't many specters brave enough to wander around the parks near the palace, considering most of those areas are a hotspot for spectral guards and those keeping their eyes out for anything unusual which might capture the queen's attention."

Carolyn huffed. "Are you saying we can't even see the sights? This is my first visit to London, and I can't visit St James's Park?"

"I'm saying those who haven't taken an oath to the queen would do well to stay as far away from her quarters as is possible. And, if my judgment is correct, you three are under no such oath."

"I can't be put under oath," Lupe told him.

Karl nodded at Carolyn and Feng Mian. "But your friends can."

Mona grinned wickedly and reached down toward her ankle, where a spectral knife was fixed with a strap. She drew it quickly and held it to Carolyn's throat.

Before it could get anywhere near her, a flash of blue sparked in the air at the point of the blade.

The knife flew out of Mona's hands and landed on the bar floor. "What the…"

Carolyn smirked. "We all have powers."

"How is that possible?" Karl turned from Carolyn to Feng Mian, whose eyes were now fixed on Mona's. "What did you do?"

Carolyn leapt off her seat and grabbed the knife. She advanced slowly on Mona with the knife held in front of her. "I think it's our turn to ask the questions. If some bitches from the paranormal court are going to try to take us down, it's best we learn everything we can about you both, don't you think?"

Karl looked suddenly afraid for Mona's safety. He waved a hand. "Okay, okay. But it's not what you think. We're not with the crown."

Mona gave him a look, then returned her attention to the knife.

"Well, we are," Karl blustered. "We're oathbound, but we're not here to capture you. We're here to help you."

"Why would you help us?" Carolyn asked.

"We heard what you did in America," Mona told them. "We want to help liberate the specters here, too."

Carolyn and Lupe turned to each other, mistrustful expressions on their faces.

"Oh, yeah?" Carolyn disputed. "Prove it."

Kensington, London

Jennie waited for the wraiths to talk first, as was customary with their kind.

There were four of them lining the chamber on either side, with one more at the end. They were imposing figures, hovering with darkness curling below them as though they were hovering on thunderclouds. Their shadowy robes moved in a breeze Jennie could no longer feel.

The wraith at the end broke the pregnant silence. His voice was breathy, a raspy hiss. "You remember the terms of our agreement?"

Jennie sighed. She'd known this would come up. "I do. I'm sorry, Canute."

"Yet, here you are," Canute intoned.

Jennie took a step forward, and every head snapped in her direction. She moved her foot back and took a deep breath. "I really meant it last time. I didn't want to see you anymore. But, do you think I would be here if this wasn't important?"

The wraith remained silent for a few seconds. It was almost impossible to tell the emotions of wraiths. Having lived alone in the crypts or stalking the graveyards, many had forgotten the ways of the mortal world, and emotions played no part in their customs.

The head wraith, Canute, snapped his fingers, and a curled piece of parchment appeared in his hands. He pointed to a section with a dark, bony finger that appeared from his sleeve. "In 1936, a pact was made. This agreement was signed by your hand. Is that correct?"

Jennie gave a curt nod.

Canute lifted the agreement and read from it. "'I, Genevieve King, do solemnly swear never to reveal the final resting place of the line of Greats. Not for aid, nor assistance, no palaver will I, willingly or knowingly allow another to enter the hall, nor will I set foot once more into the crypt.' It's all here. Signed and scripted by your hand."

Jennie winced. "I understand that, Canute. But…"

Canute cut her off with a wave of his hand. "Do oaths mean nothing to you, King?"

Jennie straightened her back and glared at the wraith. Her voice rose and echoed around the chamber. "Does loyalty and honor mean anything to you, *sir*?"

Baxter let out a small sigh and muttered, "Please don't anger it."

Jennie continued, "I understand I am here against the terms of the pact I signed. I understand the risks I am taking here. But do you not recall the deeds I performed at a time when the Wraiths of Great were in a dire situation and needed saving?"

Jennie took a step forward and now ignored the wraiths staring back at her. She could feel eyes she could not see, and there was a power in the chamber she could not describe—a presence of something larger and greater than the wraiths in the room.

"When you needed someone to stand for you, all those years ago, I was there, and I stood for you. I didn't ask why. I didn't care for a reason other than it was the right thing to do. Now a situation has arisen, and I need your abilities. Wraiths are the masters of the invisible, and it is that skill I need to harness for a task which *must* be completed."

"Why should we care for the trials of the spectral world?" a wraith to her right hissed. "What business is this of ours?"

"We serve no master. We know no bonds," another spoke.

"Because the spectral world above is on the brink of anarchy," Jennie told them.

A wraith laughed, the sound like a smoker's cough. "What else is new?"

Jennie reined in her temper. "Because your intervention could prevent an all-out war across the spectral world. Some information has come to light that I believe will greatly affect your decision in this matter. Information concerning Queen Victoria, and her rule over the paranormal court."

Now the wraiths all turned to her with interest.

Jennie smiled. "I thought that might get your attention."

Jennie briefly explained to the wraiths the situation with the paranormal court and the lies the queen had been telling throughout the years. She told them of the battle in New York and her purpose in England now. How she was being targeted by the queen's people, and she would do whatever it took to get an audience with the queen and fix what had been broken.

When she was finished, she waited for a response from the wraiths.

"You must allow us our own parley," Canute told her.

The instant Jennie agreed, the wraiths vanished into thin air. She felt them flutter by as they exited the chamber and left Jennie and Baxter behind, the sudden gust extinguishing several of the candles.

Jennie glanced at Baxter. "They're discussing it. At least that's something."

Baxter chuckled. "They're usually not so welcoming?"

Jennie shook her head. "You laugh, but this is the most welcoming they've ever been. You should see them when they're hostile."

"I'd rather not." Baxter turned back to the wall the wraiths had disappeared through, checking that they weren't listening in. "What was that contract, Jennie? You've had dealings with these wraiths before?"

"Many years ago," Jennie confirmed. "A simpler time. They asked for a favor, and I helped, no questions asked."

"And promised you'd stay away forever?" Baxter asked.

"Yeah," Jennie replied. "Not my best agreement, considering how valuable they could be in all of this."

"Valuable how?" Baxter shook his head. "All I can see are spooky Halloween specters who look like the grim reaper and have a reluctance to help those around them. They've been buried down here for years, why would they care about the surface world?"

"I have my theories," Jennie replied ominously. "Besides, in case you didn't know, wraiths have an uncanny ability to turn invisible and vanish onto a plane undetectable by other specters. That skill would definitely be useful given our task ahead."

Baxter pawed at his eye. "Couldn't you just use Rico? He had that ability, too."

"Yeah, that was a strange one," Jennie mused. "I've never seen that ability in a specter who wasn't a wraith. It's hardly like we can use him, though, is it? Not only is he ludicrously bound to the crown, but he's half a world away. I'm not in the business of dragging hostages around for the sake of it. That would make me no better than the scum I clean up most of the time."

Baxter grinned. "It would be fun to do. Wouldn't it?"

Jennie rolled her eyes, but her smile stayed on her face.

A few minutes later, the wraiths came back into the room as a rush of wind and materialized like impossible shadows.

"Well?" Jennie asked optimistically. "What's your verdict?"

Canute shook his head. "Your quest is of no benefit to the Wraiths of Great. Your request has been denied."

Jennie's jaw dropped. "You're kidding me? After everything I told you, you're going to sit down here and do nothing? You're going to waste away in the crypts and let chaos reign above?"

"We have had our day, mortal," Canute replied. "Our interest lies down here, with the others of our kind. Family is of the utmost, and there is no family for us anymore on the surface world."

Jennie was speechless for a moment. "But—"

"Leave us in peace." Canute's order came out as a blast of sound that echoed around Jennie and Baxter at an unbearable volume.

Jennie clapped her hands to her ears and attempted to latch

onto the wraith in a desperate attempt to stop what she knew was coming. She sensed his power as a great black orb of energy, but she was already too late.

The shadows of the wraiths grew into one large smoky mass that whirled around the room like a tornado. The wind whipped Jennie's hair about, and Baxter held her arm for dear life as the walls of smoke closed in.

The room disappeared in an instant, replaced with the bright blue of the afternoon sky in the next moment. The wind vanished as quickly as it had come, and everything was quiet.

Jennie raised her fist at the mausoleum entrance. "Cowards!"

Then she stormed away.

CHAPTER EIGHT

<u>**Covent Garden, London**</u>

Jennie stood at the large bar counter and vigorously shook the cocktail shaker. The repetitive action was satisfying. The ice inside rattled and drowned out the thoughts in her head.

"You shake that thing any harder, you're going to break it," Baxter warned.

"I don't get it," Jennie pondered aloud, moving to stand right next to Baxter. The cocktail shaker's exterior flicked beads of condensation. "It doesn't make any sense. Why would they refuse?"

Baxter wiped the condensation from his cheek. "Other than the fact they've got a signed paper saying they'll never have dealings with you again?"

Jennie's arms lowered, her eyes flashing with anger. "I don't need a literal answer, Bax."

"Well, I didn't need a shower," Baxter replied.

Jennie opened the shaker and poured the liquid inside into a long glass. There wasn't meant to be that much froth in a Pina Colada, but Jennie was past caring. She just needed something to take the edge off her anger and confusion.

She took a sip through her straw. "They know I can end their pitiful existence with a snap of my fingers."

Baxter frowned. "How do you kill wraiths?"

"Just like that." Jennie snapped her fingers. "Poof. Gone."

Baxter cocked his head and shuffled sideways to allow Jennie to sit beside him. "Have you somehow mastered exorcism in the thirty seconds we've been apart since this journey started?"

"Hey, I'll have you know Sandra taught me some of her skills," Jennie replied.

Baxter chuckled. "Oh, really? Enough to kill a specter?"

Jennie glanced away. "In theory."

Baxter threw his arms up, then relaxed them on the back of the couch. "I still don't get why the wraiths were so vital to your plan? So what if they can turn invisible? I saw you defeat dozens of specters in the subway. Remember? With powers like that, they stand no chance."

Jennie shook her head. "That was an untrained group of wannabe rebels. They'd been together for a few weeks—a couple of months, tops. The paranormal court has been around since the turn of the millennium, and they have the training to show for it."

Baxter had an idea of what that meant. "Damn."

Jennie nodded. "Yuh-huh."

Baxter tried his best to think of a solution, his brow creasing with concentration. "What if we find another specter with invisibility?"

Jennie stared down her nose at him. A lock of synthetic hair fell onto her face, and she took the whole wig off. "We've been through this. Name one."

Baxter could only think of Rico. "Er…"

Jennie shrugged. "Exactly. The wraiths' power is invaluable. Unless we can find something else even semi-useful, we can't get near them."

"Shit," Baxter cursed. "We've reached a stalemate."

"Not exactly," Jennie replied.

He frowned. "What do you mean?"

"A stalemate implies neither party can advance," Jennie told him. " As far as I'm concerned, the court is still working toward hunting me down. They haven't been slowed." She glanced at the clock on the wall. "And by the looks of it, they may also have our only three allies. Shouldn't they be back from their reconnaissance by now?"

Baxter was alarmed to see it was approaching the evening. The others had been gone most of the day. Surely Lupe would need to come back soon to grab some food and rest?

"Yes, it looks like it might already just be the two of us," Jennie murmured.

"Don't forget me, Rogue."

Jennie and Baxter sat up and turned around, alert to invaders in her home. She breathed a sigh of relief when she saw the fresh-faced diplomat standing in the doorway with a broad smile on his face.

"You were right," he told her, a small laugh escaping him. "You were right."

Westminster, London

"I don't like this," Carolyn muttered to Lupe and Feng Mian. "I don't like this."

Karl and Mona led the trio down the narrow streets of London. They were far from the beaten track, and the walls closed in on them, making Carolyn feel claustrophobic. It was dark out, and the shadows grew. Along the way, they passed dozens of storefronts, small, independent stores that sold fringe items like flowers and herbs, vaping equipment, antiques, books. All the stores were closed and locked up for the night.

Hardly a soul came past. Carolyn occasionally glanced from Lupe to Feng Mian, wondering what the hell they were even doing heading to a part of the city they didn't know with these strangers. She didn't know much about the spectral world, but she had learned enough to say with conviction that specters put a lot of stock in trusting other specters.

"Relax," Lupe assured her. "If things go badly, we'll be okay. We owe it to Jennie to see what these guys have to say."

"These guys were *following* us, Lupe," Carolyn hissed. "What clearer sign do we have that we shouldn't be here with them? Let's just ditch them and run. They're not even looking at us, and they'll never know."

She was right. In the last fifteen minutes, Karl and Mona hadn't turned around once. It was as if they just trusted the trio to follow them.

"What do you think, Feng?" Carolyn asked.

Feng Mian shrugged and remained silent.

Carolyn sighed. "Great."

"If they were so bad, why didn't they draw the attention of the queen's men to us?" Lupe was slightly out of breath, his short legs struggling to keep up with everyone else. "They had us dead to rights. They could've just taken us in the park, alerted the rest of the troops, and had us. I don't know where they're taking us, but I don't think they're lying."

Carolyn stared daggers at the back of their heads. "We'll see."

The moonlight bathed the streets in a mystical glow. Occasionally the light from someone's bedroom would illuminate a stretch of street. Carolyn kept as close to the shadows as possible, only stopping when Karl and Mona paused at a junction and peeked around the corner.

"The crown," Karl mouthed, and nodded at the corner.

Carolyn became aware of the glow of a group of specters as they walked nearby. Ice ran down her spine. They couldn't afford to get captured. Jennie needed them!

To her surprise, before they came into full view of the loyalist group, Karl and Mona ran ahead hand-in-hand. They stood on the far side of the group, meaning the specters had to turn away to talk to Karl and Mona.

"Splendid seeing you all, ladies and gentlemen," Karl called in a thick English accent. "Wonderful night, isn't it?"

Mona allowed a specter with a large stomach and a monocle to kiss her hand.

"It certainly is, Karl," a woman with a thick bush of brown hair agreed. "Although, I'm surprised to see you both on this side of town. I thought we had to stick to our positions since the court went on lockdown?"

Karl laughed and waved a hand. "You're absolutely right, Deidre. It's just, we're on orders, right now. It turned out South-side is actually low on ammunition. You know Thomas. He got us out of bed and told us to run over to central and acquire some stock. So, here we are." He bowed low.

"Out of ammo already?" the monocled specter asked suspiciously. "What the bloody hell have you been using it all on?"

Karl put his hand on Monocle's shoulder and used it to lean on to laugh. He raised his head and made eye contact with Carolyn and Lupe, giving a gentle nod with his head. "Go. Hide," he mouthed.

"It's a funny story, Franklin," he told the specter. "One which I don't have time to tell you in full. Suffice it to say, our new recruits have been slightly trigger-happy in their training this time around."

Franklin gave a satisfied nod. "Blasted recruits. No respect for our resources until it's been drilled into them. Tell you what, Karl. Next time I see you, I'll be sure to lay down the law on the hatchlings. Tell them what's what. Thomas may be good enough to sniff out the enemy, but he has no clue when it comes to teaching civilians how military life works."

"Oh, so true," Karl agreed, slapping his shoulder and dragging Mona around to the back of the group with him. "Ah, well. Sorry to break up this little catch-up, but we do have things to do. We'll be sure to be in touch soon. Maybe you and Lisa can come around when this has all blown over and we can get lunch."

Franklin gave a hearty laugh, cheeks coloring red. "Lunch! Good one!"

Karl and Mona slipped away to the next street where Carolyn, Lupe, and Feng Mian were waiting.

"Nice cover," Carolyn praised.

"Maybe that'll help with your trust issues," Mona smirked, hiking her cocktail dress off the floor and meeting stride with Karl.

"Depends on what lies ahead," Carolyn told her.

"Well, good thing we're here then, isn't it?"

As they rounded the corner, Karl held up the hatch to an underground entrance, something that reminded Carolyn of the entrance to a storm shelter.

Mona raised an eyebrow. "You know we can just float through, darling?"

Karl pointed at Lupe. "Not with that one."

"Oh, you're right." Mona chuckled. "I forgot you weren't one of us."

As Karl ushered them down the hatch, Carolyn caught the whisper of his words. "Oh, darling. No one else is quite like us."

A wooden staircase led them down into the basement of the building. There was a smell of dust in the air, and the lingering stink of rotten fruit. Karl and Mona took them through a back door, then through a series of interconnecting chambers until they were lost in the labyrinth beneath the street.

How many hidden tunnels and pathways does London have? Carolyn thought back to what Jennie had told them about London's secret history. She knew it had been the heart of England for centuries. But how many hiding places were there below the thriving city where bankers and lawyers sat on their thrones in high-rise buildings and the streets were flooded with traffic? She wished she knew.

Karl paused outside a door with several padlocks. "I'm sorry, mortal. This is as far as you can tread. Your specters must come with us."

Lupe's eyes narrowed. "You best be kidding, asshole."

They held each other's gaze for a long moment before Karl's face softened and he broke into laughter. "Of course, hold on."

Karl floated through the door, and a second later, the handle shook. The sound of unlocking came through, and the door opened for him. "There, see? We're all good."

Lupe strode past him and into the room.

The room was small, with nothing else inside other than a heavy-looking wooden chest, and a round metallic grate on the floor. Karl and Mona stared expectantly at the lid of the grate.

"Are you kiddin' me?" Carolyn exclaimed. "How much farther are you taking us? You're leading us into a trap, aren't you?"

Karl and Mona shook their heads. "It's just down there, I promise you. Open the lid, head on down, and all will be revealed."

Carolyn looked hesitantly at Lupe. "What do you think?"

Lupe considered the grate for a moment before shrugging. "I think I built an army of specters in an abandoned subway line. This is as good a place as any for the Brits."

"There, see?" Karl urged brightly.

"We'll see."

Lupe raised the lid off the grate, and the air from the hole gasped into the room. A small ladder was revealed. He heard mumbling from below, along with shuffling and the sound of footsteps.

Lupe turned and made his way down the ladder, using his phone screen to light the way as best as he could.

When he reached the bottom, Carolyn and Feng Mian jumped down, landing silently beside him.

All the noises stopped. The silence pressed in on them.

As far as Lupe could see from the faint light of his phone screen, there were no walls nearby. No doors, no furniture, nothing.

Metal grated across the floor above, and darkness began to close in.

Lupe was alarmed to see Karl was pushing the grate back over the hole. "You son of a bitch!" he shouted, rapidly climbing the ladder.

But it was too late. Something heavy was dragged across the floor, followed by a heavy thud.

Lupe couldn't lift the grate.

"Oh, great!" Carolyn exclaimed.

"Is that meant to be a joke?"

Feng Mian appeared at the bottom of the ladder and began to climb. He passed through Lupe and was nearly at the top when a pair of hands came out of the shadows. The assailant dragged him off the ladder and dropped him to the floor.

Lupe jumped down to check on him. Carolyn also rushed to his side. Feng Mian had a sinking feeling. Although they couldn't see them, they were all aware of specters watching them from the darkness.

"Who are you!" Carolyn shouted.

Dark chuckles were their only response.

CHAPTER NINE

Westminster, London

Pain blossomed on Carolyn's face. She could sense specters all around her, although she had no idea how many there were. She spun on her heels and another fist connected with her temple.

"Fighting in the dark? Real brave—" She cut off as another fist connected.

Beside her, Feng Mian grunted as one of their number attacked him. Or many of their number. It was impossible to tell.

"Show your faces!" Carolyn demanded, holding her arms up to guard her face against the blows.

Someone lit a match nearby, and the room was thrown into a glum light. There was a little over a dozen of them gathered around the trio in a wide circle. One of them stood closer than the rest, nursing his fist.

Carolyn's breath caught in her chest. The match was extinguished, and darkness took hold once more. What she had seen had to have been impossible. Every last one of their enemies looked perfectly identical. Every last one of them bore an uncanny resemblance to Karl.

Another blow connected and Carolyn swung her arms wildly in the darkness, hoping to hit something. Anything.

She spun at a sense of movement behind her, but just before the fist connected with her again, a flash of blue light lit the room and the specter was deflected by Feng Mian's shield.

"Thanks," Carolyn uttered, thrown off by what she was seeing. In that unexpected flash of light, each specter had their own identity. She saw men and women and teens, fat and thin, short and tall, each from different time periods.

What the fuck is going on?

Another specter came at her, and there was another flash from Feng Mian. This time, Carolyn was ready. She caught the bewildered specter in a headlock, spun behind him, and held his throat tight.

She had no idea what she was doing; it was all instinctual. Holding tightly, she slammed him to the ground and hooked a fist around, smacking the guy in the cheek continually. "Let's make this even, shall we? One. Two. Three. Ah, how's four for luck?"

"They weren't all me, bitch," the specter managed between blows.

Carolyn laughed. "Still, you're the only one I have right now, so lucky you! You win the bonus prize."

When she punched the specter, Feng Mian's shield flashed around her as the other specters joined in to try to save their friend. Carolyn waited until the specter went limp, then used the flashes to navigate her way back to Feng Mian, who was now defending both himself and Carolyn from the attack.

Lupe stood near the ladder, swinging the pistol in his hand around the room. The weapon was about as useful as a dead fish at this point. It's not like he had Jennie's abilities to make the bullets hurt specters.

Another match was struck, and once again, every specter took on the same form, only this time they became Mona. Carolyn looked into the flawless faces of over a dozen specters attacking her in cocktail dresses. The specter she had left on the floor now matched her form, too.

"What the hell is going on?" she shouted into the darkness when the match was extinguished. The effect was disorienting, to say the least.

Carolyn grew angrier by the second. The blue flashes from the shield came rapidly as strobe lights as the specters increased the frequency of their attacks on Carolyn and Feng Mian.

"Come closer. Now," Feng Mian called, his voice unusually calm, given the situation.

Lupe and Carolyn gathered themselves to him. The specter attacks were unrelenting. Faces flashed all around them as the attackers were bounced back by Feng Mian's shields.

Occasionally Carolyn and Feng Mian managed to punch and damage one of the loyalists, but was it enough?

"Hold tight," Feng Mian muttered, and for the first time since Carolyn had met him, anger crossed over his face. He closed his eyes and took a deep breath, muttering words in a language that sounded like Chinese. When he was done, he opened his eyes, thrust out his hands, and shouted, "*Obake!*"

The shield materialized around them in a glow of blue. Now the entire room was lit, Carolyn saw they were in a space that was easily the size of a modest house. The specters surrounding them gasped as the shield pulsed outward in waves of ghostly blue, each pulse pushing them back until they were sitting on the floor pinned to the walls.

Cries of distress rang out across the room. Carolyn watched without pity as the crown specters struggled to escape with each new pulse of spectral energy.

"Okay, enough!" Karl cried.

Feng Mian cut off his attack.

A match lit at the far side of the room, and Karl and Mona, looking disheveled and exhausted, advanced toward them with crooked smiles on their faces. "Enough, please. You've proven yourselves."

"*We've* proven ourselves?" Lupe grunted. "*We've*… It was *you* who were supposed to be proving yourselves to *us*, and all you've done is taken us captive and attacked us."

He aimed his gun at the specters, but they showed no signs of fear.

"That's an impressive power," Mona remarked to Feng Mian in awe. "Shields. I've not seen anything like that before in my life."

"It has been a long time since I've encountered an *Obake*." Feng Mian gave a curt bow.

"What are you talking about?" Carolyn asked. "What's an *Obake*? Who are you guys?"

Karl nodded at someone in the corner, and a specter came out of the shadows and walked around the room to light the candles. The flickering light took the edge off what had felt like a warped scene from a movie just moments ago.

"*Obake* is a traditional Japanese term for shapeshifters," Karl explained. "It is a word I have not heard in years, but one which rings with truth all the same. The *Obake* are shapeshifters. Specters with the ability to morph and take on the form of those around us. Those who we wish to represent and mimic as we go through the after-life."

"Oh…" Lupe muttered.

"What?" Carolyn asked, still confused by the whole thing.

Lupe looked hard at the couple. "These are not your true identities, are they Karl? Mona? Those specters we saw outside. You tricked them, didn't you?"

Karl grinned and transformed before their eyes. His sunglasses remained, but his stubble disappeared even as his bone structure shifted, and standing before them was a clean-shaven man with a square jaw and a wide nose. His clothes shifted, too, and now he wore a dark tracksuit stained with blood.

The woman in the cocktail dress and high heels was also now gone, and in her place was a woman with dark skin and a head of tight brown curls. She wore a pencil skirt and a shirt with flowery cuffs.

"Guilty," Karl grinned.

"Guilty," Mona echoed.

"Your real names?" Lupe asked.

Carolyn rubbed her brow. "Their names are fake, too?"

Karl chuckled, then held out his hand to Lupe. "Nice to meet you. I'm Angus Connor."

"Paige Turner," the woman offered.

"Paige Turner?" Carolyn repeated skeptically. "As in, you turn pages really fast? You've got to be friggin' kidding me. Have I just fallen into a dream? What the fuck is all of this?"

"Sorry for the ruse," Angus told them. "But we are a group of specters living outside the law. For the last few decades, Paige and I have been searching the city for others like us. Specters who have the ability to shapeshift and can use our talents for good. We are the only members of an ancient order passed down from our forebears in Japan."

"Neither of you looks Japanese," Lupe pointed out.

Paige rolled her eyes. "It's not a case of genetic heritage. *Obake* is a rare ability that originated in Japan but has spread across the world. It's incredibly difficult to find another who can shapeshift, but it's a skill which has proven itself to be useful."

"We've *seen* things," Angus told them.

"What kind of things?" Lupe asked.

"Hold on!" Carolyn rubbed her cheek, the memory of the attack still fresh on her face. "You attacked us, remember! Why are we even standing here listening to you?"

Angus' regret was clear, as was his resolve. "We had to know you could take care of yourselves. *Obake* are incredibly rare, and we need those with us who can defend and protect themselves as well as help us. Specters who can hold their own. In case you haven't noticed, things are getting tense out there. The last thing we need is to be carrying around liabilities in our order."

Carolyn considered this. While it wasn't the friendliest introduction, she certainly understood the need to ensure that people could look out for themselves, particularly in these times.

"But why us?" she asked. "There are hundreds of specters out there, and you've picked *us* to introduce to your super-secret order of the *bukake?*"

"*O-ba-key*," Angus corrected. "And it's two-fold, really. Number one, you guys clearly aren't in any way associating yourself with those bastards in the Winter Court."

"And, number two," Paige finished, pointing at Lupe, "do you understand how rare it is to find a conduit these days? The only known conduit to have existed in London for the last several centuries has been…"

"Rogue," Carolyn finished.

"Exactly. And she's not exactly what you'd expect from a typical conduit."

Lupe examined himself, clearly unsure whether to take offense or not. "Thanks?"

"Okay." Carolyn waved a hand then pinched the bridge of her nose. "So, let me get all of this straight. You guys are some weird, secret order of the *Obake*, and you're hiding down in tunnels because you don't want to be found by the Winter Court. You can all shapeshift, and you decided to bring us down here to introduce you to your order because we have a conduit. I'm guessing you want a favor from us somewhere along the line, because why else would you drag us all the way down into your super-secret dingy labyrinth if you just wanted to say hi?"

"You can breathe now," Lupe told her.

Carolyn bent over and took a deep lungful of air.

"You're right. We do need something," Angus admitted. He turned back to the others and whether or not he could tell them their secret.

"What is it?" Carolyn interrupted. "I don't want to be rude, but I'm already growing tired of this, and we've got someone expecting us back any time soon. So if you could just…" She clapped her hands twice. "Chop, chop."

Paige chuckled. "I like her."

Carolyn rolled her eyes. "Oh, well, in that case," she exclaimed, putting a hand to her chest. "Why don't we just go along with whatever plan you have in mind. I'm sure it won't be dangerous."

Paige grinned at her sarcasm. "Anyway, we need help in acquiring an artifact—something that was taken from our people long ago."

"Oh, here we go," Lupe groaned. "I thought I'd escaped the artifact hunters in America, and now we're straight back to *Tomb Raider*."

"Have you played it?" Carolyn asked. "It's an amazing game."

Lupe shrugged. "Played the first one, lost interest."

Carolyn recoiled in horror. "What! *How*? The new ones were fantastic."

Paige looked at them both as if they were speaking in Latin. "When you're both done…"

Carolyn smirked. "Right, sorry. Tell us about your quest thingy. Magical item, whatever."

Angus picked up the explanation. "It's a saber that has the ability to end the lives of specters with a single cut. Since it is imbued with the power of the exorcism rite, this sword is legendary. It is kept under lock and key at the home of a collector in London. His mansion is impenetrable to mortals, but not for specters."

"Then why do you need us to go there for you?" Lupe asked. "If it's not impenetrable for specters, and you're all able to morph into whatever the fuck you like, then why don't you all go down there and just grab it?"

"Because a curse has been laid on the weapon," Angus replied. "The sword is able to end the reigns of kings and queens. Therefore, when its power was discovered and made public, a curse was laid on the saber to enforce that no specter should ever lay hands on it again. Even those specters who have a solid grasp of material objects can never touch the blade. It is only to be kept in the hands of the mortals."

Lupe sighed. "I see. So, it's my job to somehow break in and collect it?"

Angus and Paige smiled and nodded.

"But even if he acquires it," Carolyn asked. "What then? How do you break the curse and make sure specters are able to once again touch the blade?"

"Oh, that's the easy part," Paige told her, turning to gesture to one of their followers.

An old woman with thin strands of gray hair and a black shawl stepped forward and drew a piece of parchment from her sleeve. "This paper contains the words to unravel the curse and release the specter from its mortal prison."

"Of course," Carolyn muttered. "A creepy witch with a spell handed down through the ages. Check."

"Hold on," Lupe argued. "You can't really expect me to break into someone's mansion and steal one of their prized possessions, can you? I'm mortal. I can talk to and see specters, but I have no powers of my own."

"Good thing we know someone who does," Carolyn cut in with a grin.

C H A P T E R   T E N

<u>Buckingham Palace, London</u>

Queen Victoria was sitting at the dressing table in her chambers when Porter Sykes knocked on the door.

She hadn't changed since her death. Her cheeks were as round as ever, her frame was large and rotund, and she wore a white lace headdress. Her dress was a black that looked more like smoke in her spectral form. A permanent scowl was fixed on her face.

"Yes."

Porter glided through the door, pausing on the other side and lacing his hands behind his back. "You asked to see me?"

Victoria swiveled in her seat and crossed her hands over her lap. She waited expectantly.

Porter growled, then relented. "Your Majesty."

Victoria smirked. "That's better. We presume your presence in our chambers means you have an update on the situation outside?" She managed to look down her nose at Porter despite the height difference. "Although judging by your current demeanor, I should go so far as to downgrade my expectations."

Porter cleared his throat and took a step forward. His eye was drawn to Victoria's bed, where a man with a dark monobrow and thick curls of chest hair lay half-in half-out of the sheets. He waved with one hand.

"Ignore him," Victoria told Porter. "Just a midnight snack."

Porter shuddered. "You are correct in your assumption. There is yet to be any sign whatsoever of Rogue. Kate and Gordon have contacted us from New York, and they've confirmed the worst. Worthington has been exorcised, and Rogue has almost certainly made her way back to England. For all we know, she's right here in the city."

Queen Victoria nodded serenely. She glided elegantly over to a cabinet against the wall and opened the doors to reveal shelves lined with various perfumes and vials of liquids.

"Do you know what this is, Porter?" she asked with a venomous smile.

Porter scowled. "I do not. I'm sorry."

"A cunning little concoction, to say the least," Victoria told him. "Something Rogue retrieved on one of her outings that has proven invaluable to my self-protection. It is useful for inflicting immense pain on anyone who dares to fail my orders."

Porter's jaw clenched. His eyes narrowed.

"Let me make you a little deal, oh faithful one," she murmured as she turned and shook the little vial before Porter. "Genevieve is certainly in London, currently seeking a way to worm her way into my quarters. I know she is, I can sense it. With all the America business, why wouldn't she be trying to add my head to her collection of those already rolling on the floor?"

Porter searched for the words to calm his queen before it was too late. "Your Majesty, Worthington…"

"*Shut up!* You'll speak when spoken to," Victoria hissed, her face turning red. "Do you think I care about any single specter? You should have told me when I placed Worthington on this mission that he would be a liability. That he would expose our ambitions and reveal what has taken *decades* to put into place. We had only just begun to train our eyes on our cross-Atlantic cousins, and already the whole thing has gone to shit."

Porter clenched his fists, wanting to shout back at Victoria, but knowing how unseemly that would be when there was company present in the room.

If we were alone right now, I'd...

Victoria paused and took a moment to take a breath. When she spoke, her voice was dark and measured. "No matter. What's done can't be undone. Perhaps let's look at this failure as a chance to further our own cause and remove the thorn which has been pressing in my side for years."

The man on the bed rolled over, his fat spilling onto the silk sheets like melted wax from a candle. He laughed excitedly. "You mean, remove her from the equation? Ha! I've never liked that bitch."

"Exactly," Victoria replied, looking at the man with longing eyes.

Porter grew queazy.

Victoria turned her attention back to Porter. "If we can find a way to destroy the invincible Rogue, then we at least stand a chance of regaining equilibrium across the court. That semi-immortal bitch has lasted a hundred years beyond her expiration date despite every attempt I've made to have her die heroically somewhere far-off, but she *must* have a weakness. There must be a way to take her down."

"You tell me what it is, and I'll deliver it," Porter told her. "I mean, she did me a favor removing Worthington from your affections, but I've never truly liked her. She's always been suspicious of our..." He paused and tried to look for the right word. "Situation."

"Oh, my dear Porter," Victoria murmured, cocking her head to the side. "You forget. You always have my affection."

She crossed the room with a desperate fury and took Porter's face in her hands. She pulled him toward her, and they kissed passionately for a few moments, their arms reaching around each other's backs as they pulled each other closer.

"Hey!" the man on the bed exclaimed. "What about me?"

Porter pulled back and glared at the man.

Victoria ran a thumb across her lip and stared into Porter's eyes. She held his head once more, her grip surprisingly strong. "Now, promise me something, Porter."

"Anything," he swore.

Victoria raised her eyebrows.

He rolled his eyes. "Your Majesty."

"Find her even if you have to go out there and hunt her down yourself. She is out there somewhere, I can feel it. Get reports from every intermediary and hunt for unusual activity. I want hourly checks on the palace until she's captured."

"Unusual activity?" the man on the bed asked. "You mean like a mortal walking around with two specters by his side?"

Queen Victoria and Porter both turned simultaneously to the man.

"What?" he asked. "I saw it earlier in the park. Weirdest thing."

CHAPTER ELEVEN

Covent Garden, London

The phone went once more to voicemail.

"Shit." Jennie was feeling some real fear creep in now. She had been trying to reach the others since they had arrived back at her place, and there was still no answer.

"Doesn't she ever sleep?" George asked Baxter while Jennie busied herself around the bar and occasionally hit re-dial on the phone.

"Oh, she does," Baxter told him. "Not as much as regular people, but if you don't give her some time alone with her blanky and pacifier, she'll get *real* cranky."

Jennie looked over her glasses at them both. "I can hear you, you know?"

Baxter grinned. "I know."

They had spent the majority of the night talking to George and discovering all they could find out about the current plans of the queen.

Stationed out in Piccadilly Square, his knowledge was fairly limited, although he did inform Jennie he had been called into the palace on several occasions recently to discuss items on the political agenda.

Even in death, politics never stopped. Although the queen reigned sovereign, many matters and decisions fell down to the Paranormal Government. These were diplomats who argued and researched the topics which most affected the day-to-day lives of specters.

Mostly these were matters of poltergeists, traitors, dealing with new specters, and sometimes turf wars. Every now and then, discussions regarding interactions with mortals within their realm would arise. These would often coincide with the adjournment of the mortal British government each year when they took their recesses from the House of Commons. Secret delegates would convene with the Paranormal Government and discuss matters arising which may affect the spectral world and vice versa.

"There was an emergency cabinet meeting last night. I'm afraid your name was brought up in the conversation," George told Jennie.

"So, the mortal government is going to be after me, too?" Jennie said. "Splendid."

George nodded solemnly. "You are a matter of international interest to the spectral world, and since you have dual citizenship, that matter also affects you in the mortal world."

"Dual citizenship?" Baxter asked.

"Existing in the mortal and spectral worlds," George clarified.

Baxter nodded. "Ah. I see. Never heard it put that way before."

Jennie stood up and rubbed the back of her neck. "Well, that's fantastic. A dual-pronged approach. They'll find us in a matter of minutes. We don't stand a fucking chance."

Baxter laughed, then trailed off when he realized Jennie wasn't joking. "Hold on, since when have you been one to look at things negatively?"

Jennie shook her head. "Didn't you hear him, Bax? It's not just the spectral world who'll be looking for us now. Police, intelligence agents, every damn fucker and his dog will be trying to sniff us out soon. If what they said to the cabinet was half as bad as I'm thinking it was…" She turned to George for confirmation.

He nodded.

Jennie sighed. "Then we don't have a shot. Don't you get it? We caused a disturbance in the US and set a sheet of smoke across the whole of Times Square—in their eyes, that's a terrorist action right there. Now they know we're gunning for royalty, and it's not just one queen who lives in Buckingham Palace. There's Elizabeth, too."

"To be fair," George interjected, raising a finger. "Queen Elizabeth is currently out of the city visiting her property in Sandringham."

He turned to Baxter. "She always goes there at this time of year. Lovely lawns, great nature walks, it really is a beautiful place to go."

Jennie looked at him incredulously. "Who cares where she is?"

George held up his hands. "I'm just saying, it'll lower *some* of the attention."

Jennie clapped her hands. "Well, there we are, then. We'll be fine. Now I won't have to go in all guns blazing, destroying every single fucker who steps in my way."

Baxter rose and grabbed Jennie's shoulders. She resisted at first, then curiosity took over and she stared into his ghostly eyes. "Jennie…" He smiled apologetically. "I'm sorry."

"For what?"

Baxter slapped Jennie hard.

His face dropped when he realized his hand had gone straight through Jennie's head without making contact.

"Are you kidding me?" she seethed, rematerializing when she let go of Baxter's energy. "Slapping me? Really?"

Baxter shrugged. "I thought it might change your state. Help you wake up and realize there's always another way around."

Jennie punched Baxter in the stomach.

He lost his balance and fell backward, thumping into the chair and nearly toppling it over. "I suppose I deserved that."

George chuckled warily.

"Surprise attacks are only ever going to end badly for the person springing them on me," Jennie told him. "I appreciate the sentiment, Bax, but we really need something to come to light. Something that'll help us bypass all the guards and sentinels and get into her chambers undetected. Without the aid of the wraiths, my options are becoming more and more volatile."

"Volatile?" George echoed. "Oh, I don't like that. I'd rather not make too much of a mess if possible."

"This whole thing is already a mess," Jennie retorted. "Didn't you get that from our talk? And, you know what? The minute they realize you're gone again, they'll be looking for you. Wondering where you've gone and getting suspicious." She ran a hand down her face.

"I don't care about that anymore," George replied hotly. "I'm with you, Jennie. I'm here to help."

"Then keep doing what you're doing," Jennie told him. "Go back to your post. If anyone asks, say you saw me, and you followed my trail but lost me. Send them off my scent and cause a disturbance. We'll figure out the rest."

George gave a slow nod, then vanished from the room.

"What about the others?" Baxter asked. "What do you think happened to them?"

"I suppose we'll find out soon enough," Jennie hazarded. "If they've been captured, the court is hardly going to keep that quiet, are they?" She grabbed a travel bottle and filled it with one of her pre-mixed cocktails. "Come on, let's get out of here. I'm going stir crazy down below."

Baxter tossed the wig over to Jennie. "Don't forget this."

She was about to place the wig back on her head when Carolyn appeared through the door with an excited look on her face. "Don't worry about that. We've got a better way to disguise yourself."

London Underground

The tube was busy, but not its usual rush-hour chaos. Beside Jennie, a man read a newspaper, two teenage girls with headphones blaring tinny music were standing nearby, and across from her, Lupe was sitting next to a man with a pocket-sized dog asleep on his lap.

Jennie nodded at Lupe. He had been staring at her in disbelief for the last half hour as they traveled from the Victoria Line to the Northern Line.

"It's getting a little old," she complained in a deep voice that was most unlike her own. "Stop staring."

Lupe didn't. Neither could Baxter, Carolyn, or Feng Mian. The specters stood nearby, invisible to everyone else around them, as did the man and woman who had introduced themselves as Angus and Paige. A tendril of energy connected Jenny to the man with the square jaw.

Jennie ducked her head forward and caught a glimpse of her reflection in the train window, the dark tunnels behind creating a near-perfect mirror.

I had no idea how good I would look as a man.

Hampstead Heath, London

They left the train station and walked through a well-to-do area of London. Roads were clean, and pavements were wide. Gardens were well-kept, and the houses here were huge compared to the tiny apartments in the inner city.

"I've always appreciated a well-trimmed bush," Angus quipped as they strode past a house with a hedge cut into the shape of a dolphin.

"These places are *niiice*," Carolyn cooed, lingering longer than the others at one particular front garden with a round fountain and flowers blooming in a variety of colors and shapes. "How much does one of these go for?"

"About nineteen million sterling," Jennie replied without hesitation.

Carolyn's jaw dropped. "How do you know that?"

"A few years back, I looked into investing in property and went shopping out this way. I decided to go for something else in the end."

"Your pad is nice," Baxter told her.

"Thanks," Jennie replied. "I wasn't angling for compliments, but okay."

Angus turned to Paige. "I'm starting to wish we'd insisted on coming inside now."

"No, you don't," Jennie replied. "If you had been brought into my place, and not kept several streets away, it's likely I would've shot you on entry."

Angus laughed.

Jennie didn't.

They came upon a house bordered by redbrick walls topped with spiked metal railings. A large, wrought-iron gate with an electric keypad was fixed in the wall. A security camera looked down from the top of the railing.

Jennie gave the place a quick search for any unwanted eyes, pleased to feel that at least at the edge of the city, security wasn't so tight.

Not that they would've recognized her, looking like a more tan version of Ashton Kutcher.

Jennie took a breath and muttered, "It's showtime."

She focused on her connection with Angus and extracted herself from his power, choosing instead to connect now with Paige.

"Ooh, that's uncomfortable," Paige exclaimed.

Angus grinned. "Tickles, doesn't it?"

"That's one word for it," Paige replied. "You know you don't have to choose a specifically gendered specter to turn into that person?"

Jennie shrugged, standing before them in the form of a beautiful woman with flowing blonde hair. Her lips were plump and red, and her mascara was smeared. She wore a close-fitting black shirt that revealed her cleavage, and denim shorts.

She pressed the button, and a screeching buzz rang out.

A few seconds later, something clicked, and a man's voice came over the speaker.

"May I help you?"

Now was the time to put Jennie's love for the theater into action. "Please, sir. I'm sorry to disturb you, but I didn't know what else to do, and now I'm... My boyfriend, he... Oh, I can't believe I'm telling a stranger this, but he...he *hit* me, and I just ran without thinking." She broke down into unintelligible sobs. "I don't suppose I could borrow your phone?"

The camera swiveled on the railing. Lupe remained on the other side of the street, hidden behind a wall with Feng Mian and Carolyn beside him.

Another few moments passed before the man replied, his voice breathy and ancient. "Of course, dear. Come on in."

The gate swung open as Jennie straightened up and wiped the tears from her eyes. The camera revolved and followed her along the path and up toward the house.

Lupe ducked close to the wall and dashed in before the gates had a chance to close, remaining out of view of the camera. He skirted the garden and looked for a location to spy on the action indoors.

The house was incredible from the outside. Jennie headed up the path with Paige and the other specters right behind her. The pristine red front door swung open to reveal a man in his late fifties, with a thick pair of glasses and swept-back, silver hair.

He wore a purple satin robe and his gray chest curls sprang out through the V below his neck. Despite the fact that it was now mid-morning and the sleepy cul-de-sac had started to wake, he was still in his pajama pants, too.

The man eyed Jennie's disguise for just a second too long. "Come in, dear," he invited. "It sounds like you've had a dreadful time."

If the outside of the house was a mansion, the inside was a palace. English oak floors ran through the place, floor-to-ceiling oil paintings lined the hallway walls. He ushered Jennie into the living room, where he motioned toward a luxurious sofa and took a seat on an armchair beside her. The living room show-cased a bookshelf that ran the length of the room and held a variety of contemporary novels mixed in with what were clearly ancient tomes.

"I can't thank you enough for this..." Jennie sniveled, looking at the man expectantly.

"Jensen." Jensen offered a hand.

"Rita," Jennie replied, ignoring the scoffs from the specters chuckling behind their hands.

Paige and Angus looked at each other, confused.

Jensen smiled. "Well, Rita. The phone is on the table beside you, feel free to make any calls you wish to. I've just put the kettle on, so I'll make us both a nice strong cup of tea to help settle those nerves." He reached over and tapped her bare thigh with his hand. They were clammy and cold. "Then you can tell me all about what happened if you want to."

He rose without waiting for an answer, his eyes lingering longer than was comfortable on Jennie's chest.

There was a look in his eyes Jennie had seen a thousand times before. Jennie instructed Baxter to follow Jensen when he left the room.

Baxter remained several paces behind Jensen as he navigated through several rooms into a kitchen larger than Baxter had ever seen.

Jensen switched on the kettle and waited, the sound of bubbling covering his muttering. "What do you know? Who needs a dating app when there's a gorgeous twenty-year-old wandering around my house?" He sneered. "Must be my lucky day."

He rooted through cupboards, found two cups, and popped a tea bag in each. Baxter waited patiently by the wall, studying every movement of the older man.

He was in decent shape. His shoulders were broad, his wrinkles were few, and his eyes were an Arctic blue that would make any lady swoon.

But that didn't counter the predatory vibe oozing from Jensen. Even less so when the man crossed over to a cupboard filled with various medicines and popped two small white capsules from their packet.

Jensen looked over his shoulder and chuckled darkly as he dropped both pills into one cup. At one point, he looked straight through Baxter, who froze despite a hundred years of death, terrified he might suddenly appear material and get caught in the act.

Satisfied he was still alone, Jensen called, "Is everything okay in there? I hope you like your tea strong."

He filled the cups with steaming water.

CHAPTER TWELVE

<u>Hampstead Heath, London</u>

Jennie held the phone to her ear and pretended someone was on the other end. She muttered phrases such as, "That'd be amazing, I can't thank you enough," and, "Honestly, Mum, I never saw it coming," while the specters got to work searching the house to find the location of the saber.

She placed the receiver down when she heard the footsteps coming down the hallway.

"Everything okay, dear?" Jensen asked, carrying a small tray with two cups and saucers and a round tin of biscuits. "Manage to get through to someone?"

"My mother has offered to let me stay with her for a while." Jennie choked up. "I can't believe it. Four years together, and I'm right back where I started. All alone..." Tears tracked down her cheeks. She couldn't believe her acting skills.

When was the last time you cried on cue? You've still got it, girl!

Jensen hopped over to sit next to Jennie and once more placed a hand on her leg. The other arm he draped over the back of the sofa behind her. "That sounds awful, Rita. The thing you've got to remember is that young lads are the same, just useless scum who are powered by nothing more than their own testosterone. You seem like a lovely young girl. You don't deserve to be treated that way."

Jennie batted her eyelashes. "You really think so?"

"I do." Jensen shuffled closer. "I know I'm just some strange old man you've happened on today, but I can tell that you're too intelligent and kind to be treated badly by someone like that."

Jennie smiled. "Thank you."

Jensen gave a warm smile in return. "You know, I have a daughter your age."

"You do?" Jennie asked.

If Baxter hadn't have been mouthing and communicating exactly what Jensen had done behind his head, Jennie might actually have believed he was a nice guy.

Jensen nodded. "I'll give you the same advice I once gave her when she was in a similar situation. Never trust men your own age."

"Oh, and I suppose men get more honest as they get older?" Jennie asked coyly, brushing a lock of hair behind her ear.

"As a matter of fact, they do," Jensen told her.

Baxter shook his head emphatically.

"You get to a certain age, and you just see the young, attractive ladies, like yourself, as one of your own kin. Girls to protect from the venomous and disgusting guys in the world." Jensen moved his arm around Jennie's shoulder and pulled her toward him. She allowed it, for now. "You'll be okay, dear. Don't you worry. We'll get you to your mother's, and you'll be okay. There's nothing more to worry about. It's over."

Jennie rolled her eyes, then pretended to cry into his shoulder. With her face pressed into his chest, he couldn't see that her features did not express the emotions she conveyed.

After a few more theatrical sobs, Jennie couldn't take the creep factor of Jensen sniffing her hair. She withdrew and wiped her eyes. "Thank you so much for your hospitality. I don't know what I'd have done if you hadn't have answered."

"Probably just tried the next house." Jensen laughed. "Here, drink up. Tea will make it all better for you." He passed Jennie her tea and then picked up his own. His eyes never left her cup as she raised the drink to her lips.

Just before the steaming tea made her mouth, something smashed in another room. Jensen's eyes went wide at the sound of broken china, and he excused himself to dash out of the room.

Jennie took the liberty of the distraction to swap over the cups and place them back on the table.

"Are you okay?" she called, walking to the hallway where Jensen was now muttering under his breath as he picked up large chunks of a broken white and blue vase. Baxter stood behind him, chuckling. "Oh, no. Was that expensive?"

Jensen glared at her. "It was priceless."

Jennie doubled down on her efforts to act like an innocent lamb. "Oh, that's good, then. Wouldn't want you to have lost something pricey."

Jensen stared up at Jennie in disbelief. "No, 'priceless.' It means so valuable that no one can put a price on it."

Jennie pretended to be shocked. "Oh. How much did it cost you?"

"£16,000."

"Wow. That *is* expensive," Jennie marveled, seeing an opportunity. "What was it?"

Jensen sighed and moved the larger chunks into a pile, leaving a track in the white dust scattered on the hardwood floor. "It was a genuine Chinese antique. This jar was from the Ming Dynasty in the fifteenth century. I had it exported from Chengdu by a contact of mine whose hobby is seeking rare and historical items." He poked the remains with his toe. "I have no idea how that would have fallen off such a sturdy base."

"Wow," Jennie moved away from the mess to look at the other

pieces decorating the hallway. "You like collecting old things, huh? You're kind of like Indiana Jones."

Jensen's face softened at that. Apparently, the secret button to winning the man's heart was to inflate his ego.

Isn't that the truth for most men?

"I don't know about that." He rose to his feet. "I'll get Cynthia to clean that up when she comes later today. How about since you are so fascinated by this jar, I give you a little tour of my collection?"

"That would be amazing," Jennie agreed chirpily. "I bet you've got some *super* rare pieces, haven't you?"

Jensen's eye twinkled. "You have no idea."

He led Jennie back into the living room, where they each grabbed their tea for the tour. While sipping their drinks, Jensen led Jennie around his house, describing the impressive collection of artifacts and souvenirs he'd gathered from a life traveling the world.

The walls were decorated with oil paintings interspersed with taxidermied hunting trophies mounted on plaques. Jennie hid her distaste at seeing the glassy eyes of various rare creatures from around the globe.

Jensen showed Jennie shelves and pedestals filled with precious objects that shone with every color of jewel and precious metal known to man. Shields, and goblets, and Faberge eggs lined the displays, which, like the rest of the house, showed not a single speck of dust.

As Jensen guided Jennie around the house, he occasionally glanced at her expectantly, then placed a hand to his head as if to soothe a headache or discomfort he couldn't quite explain.

After around fifteen minutes or so, they reached the end of the tour around the first and second floors, finally. Jensen wobbled on his feet as they made their way back downstairs into the hallway, clutching the banister for support.

Jennie smirked. "Wow, who would have known that when I rang your doorbell, I'd be taken around the world in eighty days."

Jensen nodded but didn't reply. All of his efforts were on concentrating on not falling.

Jennie moved closer, giving her hips a little extra wiggle as she did. She placed a hand on his cheek and kissed the other. "I can't thank you enough for showing me your collection. Do you feel a little bit drunk, maybe?"

Jensen gave her a strange look as if trying to work out what had gone wrong with his plan and if maybe he had placed pills in both drinks.

Jennie wobbled a little in front of him, allowing her eyelids to droop until they were half-closed. She'd had enough experience being drunk to know what it was like to look as though you'd lost your inhibitions.

Jensen smirked goofily. "That's not all, you know?"

"No?" Jennie stared deep into his eyes.

He shook his head. "I have a hidden collection. Follow me."

Using the wall to remain upright, Jensen moved to a small cupboard under the stairs. There was a keypad there, which he typed a six-digit code into. A hydraulic lock -clicked, and he opened the door to reveal a set of fluorescent lights that flickered into action.

Jennie bit her lip and allowed herself to be ushered inside.

Yeah, follow the creepy old man into the locked cupboard under the stairs to discover his "hidden collection." If this isn't a commercial for stranger danger, I don't know what is.

Lupe strained his neck to see through the window. The exposed parts of his skin were now covered in tiny scratches from the rose bush where he was crouching with Carolyn.

Another thorn prodded into his ankle. "Ow, fuck."

"Quit complaining," Carolyn whispered. "Pain doesn't last forever."

"Easy for you to say," Lupe hissed. "I wish I could float inside a bush and not feel the thorns and spikes."

"Just concentrate," she told him.

They had watched as Jennie was led out of the room by the old man. The minute she was out of sight, Lupe began to grow concerned.

They trailed her around the house as best they could. Feng Mian was their eyes and ears, trailing into the house, and then back outside to provide progress reports.

"Still no sign of the saber?" Lupe asked, feeling useless.

Feng Mian shook his head.

Lupe picked a thorn out of his cloak. "Judging by the way the old man was drinking that tea, it won't be long until he's out cold."

"It's the least he deserves, the animal," Carolyn added.

They resumed their position near the front of the house when the old man thumbed the keypad and opened the door of the under stairs cupboard. Lupe watched with distress as the old man gestured for Jennie to take the lead into the room, his eyes lingering on her ass as she walked ahead of him.

"I need to get inside." Lupe leaned out of the bush and looked at the door. "I bet that fucker has it alarmed."

"We don't know the code," Carolyn told him. "You're going to have to stay outside, pal."

Lupe shot her a look. "Excuse me?"

Carolyn shrugged. "Well, it's not our fault you're mortal, is it? We'll go ahead and check that she's okay. No point in Jennie risking any undue suffering because you're too selfish to stay hidden and set off the alarm."

"Since when was it considered bad to be mortal?" Lupe argued.

Carolyn tilted her head. "I'm not saying that. I'm saying

rushing in and endangering Jennie just because you're feeling less than useful would be selfish."

Lupe crossed his arms, his dark eyes flashing. "If I could go spectral, I would be useful."Carolyn lifted her hands. "What do you want me to say? If wishes were fishes, you'd be stinking."

Lupe opened his mouth to argue, but before he could, there was a long, low beep. The lights in the house flickered momentarily, then came back on.

Carolyn and Lupe both turned toward the front door where Feng Mian stood in the open doorway. He gave them a placid look and said, "Scrambled the circuits. Come."

Lupe glared at Carolyn. "Was that so hard?"

Once, long ago, Jennie had been invited to visit a Saudi prince's palace. This was not long after the Second World War when Western Europe was recovering from years of depression and rationing, and Jennie was given a rare break.

She had been in pursuit of some answers about her past. Some inclination of what heritage she bore that had gifted her the powers she possessed. Her hunt led her halfway across the world.

Prince Hasan el-Guler saw her in the souk and was so taken by her beauty he had ordered his men to bring her to him. Jennie had gone along with the request out of a mixture of curiosity and amusement, and the prince had delighted in showing her his collection of strange and exotic trinkets he had acquired throughout the years.

Jensen's hidden collection was nothing like Prince el-Guler's.

This room was wall-to-wall painted concrete rather than the gold-threaded marble she remembered from the prince's palace. Metal pedestals held glass boxes containing diamonds and jewels that were impressive in size. She dismissed the scythes, axes, and daggers decorating the walls.

Jennie found the comparison laughable.

How the Western world butchers the magnificent.

Jennie strode up to the nearest pedestal, leaning closer to explore the diamond inside. The metal glinted when the LED spotlights flickered off for a moment before restoring light to the room.

"This thing is bigger than my fist," Jennie remarked to distract Jensen from the power surge.

"Mm-hmm…" Jensen shook his head, struggling to focus his eyes. There was a thin film of sweat on his head. "The third-largest in the world… Well, found so far."

Jennie forced an interested smile, hoping he would pass out soon. "Impressive. And this one?"

"That's the ruby necklace Edward gives Vivian in *Pretty Woman.*"

Jennie took a step back and cocked her head.

Jensen smacked his lips together. "What? I'm a fan."

Jennie turned to the pedestal in the center of the room. The one her eye had caught immediately, but she didn't want to draw attention to her interest. Angus and Paige stood by the saber with a hungry look on their faces.

"What's this?" she asked lightly.

The saber was long, its razor-sharp edge glinted in the light. The handle was polished gold with emeralds embedded in the pommel. It stood upright, connected to a long metal rod by a series of small wires.

"Ah, a woman of fine taste." Jensen coughed, made to move toward Jennie, and stumbled over his own feet, stopping himself falling at the last minute. He looked at Jennie. "Do you feel funny?"

"Where's it from?" she pressed, ignoring his question. "It's beautiful."

"That one's an incredibly rare specimen." Jensen now leaned on Jennie's shoulder. "I spent years tracking down the *Divinitatem Sancti Machaera*."

Jennie's eyes widened. "Excuse me?"

"The Saber of the Holy Divinity," Jensen translated, his words starting to slur as his eyes closed. "Legend has it this blade was made in 36AD. Imbued with the light of the nine holy brothers of Bahá'í, this is said to be *the* unbreakable saber. The blade no barrier can stop."

"Wow." Jennie reached out for the sword and ran two fingers along the flat of the blade. It was cold to the touch, but the metal thrummed with an ancient power deep.

She grazed her fingers on the blade, and immediately small lines of red rivulets of blood appeared. She retracted her hand quickly and dabbed the blood on her clothes.

"So sharp!" she marveled, more to herself than to Jensen. "Of all the swords I've seen in my lifetime, of all the blades which were rumored to have been cursed, magical, or powerful, only a few have truly fit the description. But you! You're the real deal, aren't you?"

A small smile played on her lips.

Jennie had always had a passion for the undiscovered treasures of the world. With the spectral world a well-kept secret from the realms of the mortals, there were thousands of powerful objects across the world kept in small closets such as these by selfish mortals who wanted to show off rare artifacts rather than use them for their purpose.

If only mortals knew the true power of some of the items they possessed...

Jennie took the hilt and gave it a gentle tug. The metal wires resisted, and the lights at the base of the pedestal turned an angry red.

She tugged again, but the blade held fast.

"Jensen, how do I remove this from its stand?" Jennie asked, already knowing what the response would be. She looked down at where Jensen had fallen asleep on the floor in the fetal position and shook her head. "At least you won't be awake to see what happens next."

She cut off her connection to Paige and returned to her normal appearance. She drew her pistol and severed the cables with two quick, well-placed shots.

He is going to be pissed *when he wakes up,* Jennie thought as she grabbed the sword and ignored the mess of shattered glass and cracked stone in the room.

"Come on, you three. Let's get the fuck out of here." Jennie turned on her heels and made it to the top of the stairs before she paused.

Baxter looked back at her from the door. "What are you doing?"

Jennie chewed her lip. "Teaching this guy a lesson. Hold on."

She rifled around in the kitchen drawers before returning triumphantly with a permanent marker in her hand. She ran down the stairs and scribbled on Jensen's forehead, leaving a message which he would wake up to and hopefully learn something from.

Let's see him explain that, Jennie chuckled and read the writing on his skin. "Rapist." A simple message for the police who would arrive shortly.

Now Jennie raced up the stairs and through Jensen's house, making it as far as the door before the blaring of police sirens could be heard from way down the street.

"You've got to be kidding me," Jennie muttered.

"The podium must have been alarmed," Paige guessed. "That would explain the red light."

"You don't say." Jennie's eyes narrowed. There was only a limited window of time for them to make a clean escape. She connected to Baxter, passed through the door and almost crashed into Lupe in the garden.

"Jennie, what's—"

"Not now." Jennie held the sword high as she ran around the house and toward a fence that bordered the back garden. There was another lock with a keypad on the gate.

"Allow me," Feng Mian offered, and the gates clicked open.

Jennie waited for Lupe to catch up, then shoved him through as she became material.

The police made it to the front of the house a few moments later.

They dashed through the gate, calling out to alert intruders to their presence, little knowing Jennie, Lupe, and their spectral friends had already hauled ass.

C H A P T E R   T H I R T E E N

<u>Piccadilly Circus, London</u>

The sky was growing darker, and George was getting bored.

How long am I going to have to stand here and just watch the world? They're out there, right now, doing something, and I'm standing and...what?

George looked out over the top of the building and wondered where Jennie was now.

It was an impossible mission, to break into the palace and get to the queen. Although he would be considered young amongst the specters, he was old enough to know it would take nothing short of a miracle to get the kind of result Jennie wanted.

"And, what then?" he muttered in the chill breeze as the sun burned a fierce orange on the horizon. "What's her plan once she's got her in her grips?"

Melissa's voice came from behind. "Got who in whose grips?"

George turned suddenly and stroked the back of his neck. "Oh, you know… Just thinking about Jade and Rachael."

"Your ex and her boss?" she asked.

"Yeah." George chuckled. "I haunted her last week. Think she's gunning for her position."

Melissa scoffed. "You really need to leave the past in the past."

George grinned. "Easier said than done. Did you want something?"

"Your shift is up. Kershaw's collecting the specters down at the Recess."

"Thank God," George enthused with a sly grin. "I thought I'd be up here for another night."

The Recess was a small underground games club located beneath a thriving gin bar. The multi-room underground complex had once been the hit of the gaming scene around the time that pinball and arcade machines were at their peak.

Kids, teens, and lonely adults from all across London would come and pay their coins to jab the joysticks and mash the buttons, each searching for the glory of putting their initials in 16-bit letters on the screen.

A decade ago, however, the owner of the bar announced its closure. Gaming had moved online, and there was less and less interest in the nostalgic feel of a night of *Frogger* and *Street Fighter*.

Little did the owner know that just a couple of years after he passed away while still in possession of the deeds to the club, retro gaming would become a multi-million-pound industry for a thriving gaming market.

George could understand why this was the perfect place for a congregation of specters to debrief and, occasionally, socialize. The space was dark and abandoned. Arcade machines rusted away under dust-covered white sheets. Old blackboards with faded chalk letters littered the walls. Cobwebs covered the stools and spaces around the room.

"Central has reported there may have been a sighting," Kershaw informed them, kicking back in a deteriorating leather armchair. "Some new blood around the Park. Think it might be something to do with her."

"It's not the cleverest idea for her to make it known where she is in the city," Melissa commented. "Surely no one is that stupid, especially when every specter in the city is hunting for her. If I was her, I'd give up and go hide in the Cotswolds. Live a quiet life away from it all. What's she in all of this for, anyway? She's human. Why doesn't she go and be human?"

"When people feel strongly enough about injustice, they put all else aside to fight it," George mumbled, his eyes widening when he realized he'd spoken aloud.

"Injustice?" Darren asked as he patted down his blood-stained hospital gown to straighten it out. "What injustice? The way I see it, it's those fucking Yanks who have caused the injustice, questioning the paranormal court like they are. The court never had these problems when spreading out to the colonies in the East. The Indians and the states around the Caribbean never argued. Straight into the court's pockets, they were. Even in death, they understand the value of serving for the bigger cause. The Yanks should have jumped on board."

Kershaw eyed George darkly. "Something you're not telling us, Wheatcroft?"

George shrugged off the comment. "Please. I'm just saying, we've seen it all through history. Some people will fight to their deaths if they *think* they're right. Doesn't matter whether that's true or not. Just look at Hitler."

"Or Saddam," Melissa agreed.

"And Jack the Ripper," Darren added.

Kershaw turned up his lip. "Jack the Ripper? We're talking real people here, not fiction."

"Jack the Ripper was real!" Darren protested. "They've got records of his crimes and everything. He wasn't some Sherlock Holmes fucker popped straight out of someone's pencil to the page."

Kershaw scowled. "Prove it."

"How am I supposed to prove it?" Darren asked.

Kershaw smirked. "Exactly."

"I bet Her Majesty would know," Melissa commented. "She's older than most of us, isn't she? Especially if you count her living years."

Darren placed a hand over his heart. "Longest-serving queen of England, God bless her soul."

"Longest reigning queen of the paranormal court, too," Kershaw added. "Impressive titles to bear."

George looked around at the group. Several other specters were now appearing around the Recess, coming off their own watch duties and meeting friends for a chinwag. He wondered whether now would be the time to test the waters.

"About that," he started, staring at the floor. "How the whole line of succession works? Like, when does the next ruler take over, and all that jazz?"

They all thought about it, then shook their heads.

"No idea," Melissa replied. "All I've ever known is Vicky— *Ow!*"

Kershaw chuckled as Melissa picked up the small square lighter he had thrown at her head. A trinket he had forgotten was in his pocket when he died, and now accompanied him wherever he went. Shame it was mostly useless in spectral form. "You watch how you address Her Majesty," he warned. "Or I'll set her dogs on you, and you'll find yourself on the other side of the fucking abyss, you got that?"

Melissa looked as if she wanted to argue but thought better of it.

They fell into a thoughtful silence, each dealing with their nerves about the unknowns to come. In the far corners, specters nattered to each other, discussing the excitement the hunt for Rogue was bringing to their sleepy organization. London city center had been something of a null zone for some years, generally speaking.

While there was news brewing of some antics across the ocean, London remained under strict rule by Queen Victoria, so

Rogue was the talk of the town. The specters—many of whom had had nothing more to do than roam London and occasionally haunt their descendants—were glad of something new to talk about.

"She's right, you know." Darren spoke up sheepishly. "All we've ever known is Victoria, but it wasn't always her, was it? I wonder when a new monarch will come in?"

Darren wilted like a plant attacked with fire when Kershaw shot him a look.

"It's not our business to know the inner workings of the court," Kershaw snapped. "It's our business to serve whoever is deemed worthy of accommodating the throne." He glared at George and Melissa. "Any more of that kind of talk, and I'll be forced to report you for seeding mutiny. You got that?"

Before they could nod their heads, voices rose behind them. A group of specters was in the middle of a heated discussion, in which one trail-away voice spoke above everyone else. "From what I've heard, he's on her track right now. Drek's got a nose for this kind of thing. I'm telling you, give it a few hours, and she'll be pretty putty in our hands."

The group exploded in raucous laughter.

Kershaw raised his head and called over to the specters. The loud-mouthed specter was a woman with broad shoulders and a heavy brow.

"Problem, Kershaw?"

"You got a lead on the girl, C?"

The woman held his gaze, a pregnant pause in the air as the others fell quiet. Her jaw clenched. She opened and closed her fists. "How many times I gotta tell ya? My name's Clandestiny. Don't fucking shorten it, okay?"

"I'm not calling you that." Kershaw chuckled. "Ridiculous name. You say you might know where she is?"

"Drek does. He's headed there right now. Spotted her not too far from here, actually. Oxford Circus. Right in the heart of human activity. Clever, really. Hiding in the open among all the other humans. It'll be like a *Where's Fucking Wally* book."

Kershaw rose to his feet. "Well, ladies and gentlemen, you know where we're going, don't you?"

Darren, Melissa, George, and the others looked at him.

Melissa groaned. "We've been on watch all night. Can't we have a few hours rest?"

"Yeah, Kershaw. Give your ladies a break. Leave all the glory hunting to the real men," Clandestiny scoffed.

Now it was Kershaw's turn to clench his fists, his inner mind battling with folly and pride. "You calling yourself a man?"

Clandestiny sneered. "I'm more of a man than you'll ever be."

Kershaw smirked. "Oh? Why don't you prove it?"

The specters around Clandestiny stepped back. Other specters in the Recess had stopped talking and now watched with quiet fascination.

"You're toast, mate," she boasted, before charging at Kershaw.

Northwest London

"Now, this is more like it!" Jennie laughed over the roar of the wind rushing through the open windows. Her GT500 sped down the dual carriageway with ease, accelerating at the touch of the pedal, braking, and switching lanes as if it had a mind of its own. The car chewed up the road as if it hadn't eaten for months.

Lupe sat in the back in between Carolyn and Feng Mian. Baxter took the front passenger seat, and Angus and Paige hovered in the gaps in-between. Although the specters were immaterial, Lupe still bunched his shoulders as if he'd been crammed in with four mortal humans.

"You might want to slow down a bit," Baxter advised. "You've only just got the car back. Do you really want it to go to the shop again if we slam into the car in front?"

"Don't forget about the cops," Lupe added.

Jennie laughed. "Come on, guys. Do you really think I haven't learned a thing or two about evading the police? I've been in this business for years, and there's no way we'll get caught. I know every camera, every hotspot, every place they try to pick up speeders." She stroked the steering wheel. "Plus, they'll never find us in my new baby."

The car was slick and looked brand-new. The garage had done a stellar job respraying the bright, gleaming red into a midnight black that didn't just reflect color but seemed to absorb it.

"All it will take is a detour down a quiet street, then turn off the lights, and the pigs will whizz right by us as if we don't even exist."

"Pigs?" Lupe asked.

"5-0," Angus replied. He frowned at Lupe's blank face. "Boys in blue? Bobbies? Peelers?"

"Cops," Baxter clarified, remembering the conversation he'd had with Jennie.

"Ignore them," Carolyn called, her head hanging out the window. "This thing is built for speed. Open the kitty up and let her purr!"

Jennie obliged, expertly navigating the roads around the outskirts of London. When they grew closer to the epicenter of London, Jennie closed all the windows, the tinted glass barring anyone's view of the inside of the car.

They slowed down significantly, joining the flow of traffic. Jennie had taken every precaution she could think of—including switching her license plate with a dummy one. They kept their eyes peeled as they drove past some of London's most prominent landmarks.

"There's a car park a little way from Westminster," Jennie told them. "We'll duck the car inside and head over from there."

When parked, Jennie latched onto Angus and disguised herself as a fifty-something man with a slight beer gut protruding through the buttons of his shirt. She was smartly dressed, with a fair crop of hair, and she kept her head up as she strolled through the alleyway and toward the hatch Angus now held open for her and Lupe.

They jumped down the hatch into the hidden lair of the *Obake* and followed the tunnel systems to a locked door, which Angus opened.

Candlelight revealed a large room. The thick layer of dust told Jennie no mortal had been there for a very, very long time.

"Charming place you've got here," Jennie remarked.

A number of specters appeared in a circle around her, each one of them an exact clone of the fifty-something man she embodied. "Oh, right."

Jennie released Angus' energy, and the room was filled with gasps of shock.

Angus and Paige calmed the *Obake* and explained Rogue was here to help them. There was some muttering among the group, and when Jennie drew the sword from her side, the room fell silent.

"Impossible," an old woman gasped, her strands of gray hair falling like cobwebs off her head.

"Not really," Jennie told her. "You've just got to know how to exploit the male tendency to think with their reproductive systems. Easy in this case, since the man was a deviant."

The woman grimaced. "You slept with the man who stole the saber?"

"Hell, no!" Jennie protested. "I'm sorry, I'm not that kind of girl. He has some explaining to do when he wakes up with a nasty headache sometime in the next few hours. Besides, it's hardly stealing if he inherited a blade which specters can't touch, is it?"

"Speaking of," Angus urged the woman eagerly. "Isn't it about time we test your enchantment and break the spell?"

Jennie placed the sword in the center of the room. She took a few steps back, and the specters joined her. They kept a respectful distance from the saber, which was known to send specters to permanent death if they so much as touched it.

The ancient woman bent over the blade and withdrew her parchment from her pocket. She muttered the words and waved her arms over the blade for tense minutes.

Jennie glanced at Baxter, eyebrow raised. Baxter shrugged. They weren't sure what to expect. Having dealt with items like this in the past, Jennie knew the reaction could be anything from a small shower of sparks to a sudden blast of energy which would wipe out everyone in the room in one go.

Though the latter had only happened once, those bastards had deserved it. Who tries to set off a bomb imbued with spectral energy in the middle of a train station?

When it was clear nothing special was happening, the old woman stepped back and scratched her head. She waved the parchment at the saber and glared at Jennie. "Are you sure this is the genuine artifact?"

"I don't know," Jennie told her acidly. "Why don't you touch it and see?"

The old woman looked like she was genuinely contemplating it for a moment. Then she threw her arms angrily into the air. The paper flew out of her hand. "I don't get it!"

Jennie rolled her eyes and picked up the paper from the floor. The spectral yellowed parchment was covered in characters from a language long lost to common knowledge.

"Don't even bother trying," the woman told her with a dismissive chuckle. "It's Latin. Only those with a classical education can read the ancient scrolls. Some twenty-something conduit doesn't stand a chance."

Several specters around the room. Those who knew the truth about Jennie's powers and life shuffled awkwardly. They knew better than to anger her.

Jennie remained calm. "I understand what it must be like to be ancient as far as mortality goes, but I'll warn you now the worst thing you can do in life is to evaluate people based on their looks." She held the parchment up and scanned the words, then turned it over and pointed to four lines of hastily written script. "Luckily for you, I'm here. This says you need a powerful conduit to provide energy for your enchantment in order to break the spell. Maybe you skipped that bit? It must have been hard to read this small writing from up on your high horse."

The woman scowled at the chuckles from the other specters and put her hands on her hips. "Very well, then. Let's try it your way."

"No," Jennie told her with a smile. "Let's work *together*. It's the only way this will work. You read the spell, and let me do my thing."

Jennie lowered herself to one knee and placed the flat of her palm against the blade. As the old woman muttered and spoke the words of the parchment, Jennie concentrated on feeling every specter in the room. She called their power to her, ignoring the gasps as tendrils of energy came forth from every specter in the room.

They snaked through the air, seeking Jennie. In the moments before they connected, she heard several exclamations and felt some of the specters resisting, terrified that in connecting to her they would be connecting to the blade, and thus be risking their lives.

But Jennie knew better than that."Relax. It's fine," she assured them.

The energy connected with her, making Jennie the axis of the circle of spectral energy. The power came alive in her body, filling her with a glowing warmth she concentrated on sending into the blade.

An electric hum filled the air as the energy connected. The specters stared wide-eyed as Jennie took a step backward and the saber lifted off the floor. Its blade and hilt glowed in a violent white light that stung their eyes as it increased in intensity with each repetition of the spell.

The old woman dropped the paper, now speaking the lines without conscious thought. After several more repetitions, the light reached a dazzling crescendo, and a blast of light exploded outwards from the saber with a final word from the woman.

The specters fell back, stunned. Lupe and Jennie were thrown to the floor.

The sword hovered, glowing in the darkness. Then they heard it clatter to the floor.

"Is it…Is it done?" Angus asked.

"Is everyone okay?" Paige asked as she felt around the room to re-light the candles. "Is anyone hurt?"

The specters confirmed they were okay as they picked themselves up off the floor and gathered around the blade.

"It doesn't look any different," Angus commented.

Jennie knelt once more and tried to feel the energy inside. "It certainly feels different. Who's going to be the first test dummy?"

The specters of the *Obake* turned to each other, every one of them excited but reluctant to be the first to risk holding the blade.

Angus moved closer to the saber. "I'll do it. I'm the leader, so it should be me who sacrifices for the ultimate weapon." His hands shook as he reached for the hilt of the sword. When he was inches away, he took a deep breath and steeled himself to pick it up.

His hand grasped thin air.

"It's mine!" the old woman shrieked, snatching the saber before Angus got to it. She held the blade high in the air and stared at it apprehensively as if she might explode at any minute.

After a few seconds, when it was clear it was safe, she swung the sword in clumsy figure-eights around her body. "Ha! It's mine! At last, it's mine!"

"Heather, what are you doing?" Paige said. "Give the blade to Angus."

"Yeah, right. As if I'm going to just hand over the ultimate weapon. You want it, come and claim it." She jabbed the blade threateningly in the air.

Angus raised his hands and paused his advance. "Heather, be careful. We're not even sure how the power of the blade works. You don't know what it's capabilities are."

Heather lowered the sword. "You're right. Here. Let's try something."

In a rapid move, Heather slashed the specter beside her. The blade cut a line from the top of his head to his stomach. White light immediately began to spill from where the sword had carved.

A second later, the specter shrieked, and white light exploded from the place where he stood. When the light had gone, so was the specter.

Heather cackled in delight while the others looked at her in horror. "There's your answer! It works! It works!"

Paige took a step forward with her palms held out. "Heather, please. What is all of this about? Why are you doing this?"

Heather's cackle turned into a long cough. She wiped her mouth with the back of her hand. "All these years roaming this Earth as a specter, searching for other shapeshifters and wondering what the hell I was and why I was so different from everyone else. You'd think being initiated into the royal order of the *Obake* would be a lifelong dream accomplished, wouldn't you?"

She looked at the others for a response but continued before anyone could speak. "*Wrong!* Do you know how long I spent wondering when my time would come? When I'd get a chance to have some kind of success? Lead a pack? Make it to the big time?

"Then I came across *you.*" She glared at Angus. "A man who squanders our powers and keeps us in these dark rooms beneath

London. You're a weed trying to lead a bushel of roses." Her voice grew louder, her words more shrill. "We could be *anything* we want! We can literally transform to whoever we want! We could sit on the queen's fucking throne, for all anyone would know. And what do we do? Take your stupid oath and rot in the dungeons below the city. Well, no more! I'm taking control of the order, and I'm spreading my wings and flying free. Who's with me?"

She looked expectantly around at the specters, but none met her eye.

"What are you talking about?" Angus said. "We never asked you to take an oath."

"Bullshit!" Heather screeched, lashing out and destroying another specter. The blinding light dazzled everyone with its intensity. "Absolute bullshit! I've got the most powerful spectral weapon in the world, and I'm going to use it. If you don't want to follow me, then fine. Fuck you all. I'm out of here."

She marched toward the far wall and raised the sword to hack at the specters in her way. A split second before the sword connected with the specters, she froze.

"What? What's going on?" Her shrill voice came out of lips that didn't move.

Jennie walked toward Heather, unafraid in the slightest. Her spectral tendril was latched onto the woman, and she knew there was no possibility her of breaking free. "You know, the only bull-shit I've heard tonight is that you've got the world's most powerful weapon."

Heather grunted and struggled against Jennie's hold. Jennie unclasped Heather's hand from the sword and took it from her, then walked back to the others and released Heather.

Heather stumbled and tried to catch herself but failed. She picked herself up and dusted herself off, now looking around the room as if seeing everyone for the first time.

"What… What just happened?" she asked, feigning surprise.

"Don't give us that shit," Jennie told her. "Get the fuck out of here before I do to you what you've done to a bunch of undeserving specters."

Heather contemplated her chances, then dashed out of the room without another word.

"Are you sure letting her go is a good idea?" Baxter asked. "What if she tells the others where we are?"

"It doesn't matter," Jennie told him, examining the saber in her hand. "The world's most dangerous weapon is now holding the world's most dangerous weapon."

CHAPTER FOURTEEN

<u>Buckingham Palace, London</u>

Victoria's ears heated as she walked along the palace corridor. Her annoyance often manifested as areas of warmth in random locations across her body, and now was no different.

"That bloody witch…" She gave a small grunt and spun the decorative vase so the pattern of the jaybirds on the willow tree faced outwards, hiding the image of the sunshine and the lake painted on the back.

"Much better," she muttered. She continued on through the palace, knowing full well that tomorrow she would have to rotate the vase again after Elizabeth awoke and shifted it back to *her* favorite side.

Death is a never-ending struggle, Victoria thought.

She met her guards at the door. Porter and Yasmine were accompanied by a dozen beefeaters who had served in life and died.

Unlike the living beefeaters, these lacked something in the way of uniformity. While they all wore their red coats and bearskin hats, each generation of beefeater's uniform was slightly altered from the last, and now the whole unit looked like they were wearing a collection of old budget theater costumes.

Luckily, that didn't make them any less intimidating to look at. Each beefeater sported a serious expression on their faces. Each one was obedient to Her Majesty's every call.

They guided her across the Birdcage Walk and past St James's Park. To spectators of the mortal persuasion, the queen's coach rolled by slowly with the curtains drawn and only one soul in sight, the coach's driver who held the reins of the horses and kept his head high as bypassers stopped and took pictures, hoping to witness a glance of Elizabeth on her travels.

Specters flooded out of St James's Park and lined the roads. When they arrived at Parliament Square, the coach took an unusual turn into the back entrance of the House of Commons through a gate that was locked tightly behind them.

The coach moved out of sight of prying eyes before the footman opened the door and allowed Victoria out of the cabin.

Victoria nodded as the footman gave her his hand to help her down. "Wonderful, as always, Jeffrey."

Jeffrey bowed low.

The evening had already grown dark, but the inside of the House was brilliantly lit. Specters lined the long benches and stood at the arrival of Her Majesty, holding their positions while she glided through and took her seat in the large chair that accommodated the speaker of the house during daylight proceedings.

Victoria scanned the room, delighting in the power she held. She remained standing in silence for several more moments than necessary before taking her seat and allowing the rest of the chambers to follow suit, signaling the start of the Midnight Council—a long and ancient tradition, in which the world under the rule of the paranormal court provided their updates to the queen and reports were made from all corners of the Empire.

The Midnight Council began as it always did, with the census of those who had died in the past month and what percentage of those had since sworn to the court.

Richard Tallon, a small, weedy man with spectacles and a high collar read the statistics, refused to meet the queen's eyes when he gave his news. "Specters taking the oath has taken a slight fall this month to 96.3% of all new specters."

Victoria pinched the bridge of her nose. "It's dropped again."

The chamber was silent. Richard swallowed hard, then stuttered. "I... It's taken a drop, yes. But last month was only 96.7%, so it's still in the high percentile of—"

Victoria slammed her fist on the chair. A small shockwave of energy pulsed through the room at the impact, eliciting gasps from several of the specters. "Last month was too low, too." She growled. "Do you think we're running some kind of hippy organization where it's okay to fail? Do you think it's okay to watch the numbers slowly drop? At the beginning of my rule, our uptake was 99.1%. That's a three-point-eight percent drop. Do you know what that means?"

Richard tried to speak but couldn't quite bring himself to correct the Queen's numbers.

Victoria continued, oblivious. "It means that for every hundred new specters, at least three of them are roaming free. Neutrals, running around in my empire." She turned to a woman standing beside Richard. "Eleanor, read the numbers again."

Eleanor demonstrated a much stronger backbone than Richard. She nodded enthusiastically, took the parchment from his hands, and read the numbers. "The total number of deaths was 40,012. The total number of new specters is 21,606. Fifty-four percent of those opted for a spectral life. Of those 21,606, a total of 20,807 have sworn allegiance to the court."

"Which leaves?" Victoria snapped, aiming her anger at Richard.

Richard performed some quick mental arithmetic, glancing occasionally at the paper for support.

"768 unassigned specters!" Victoria shouted before he could finish.

"Actually," Eleanor whispered, "it's 799."

"768 specters!" Victoria repeated. "That's almost eight hundred specters roaming around England and *not* dutifully obeying the rules of the court. *My rules*. I cannot allow this. Who's in charge of the oathing team these days?"

A tall black woman with round glasses and a ghostly briefcase stood up and raised her hand. "Willow Harden, Your Majesty."

Victoria appraised her a moment. "I want your people working harder out there to ensure the rates rise. Round up any neutrals across the country and bring them around to taking the oath. Get them indoctrinated into the court. If you need more specters, fine. I'll give them to you."

Willow nodded. "Understood, Your Majesty."

"Also, assess the indoctrination process," Victoria added as an afterthought. "If they're not choosing the oath, I want to know why. Collect all the data you can and return next month with a better result. I will not stand for this sort of insubordination."

"Understood." Willow nodded, then resumed her seat.

Victoria nodded. "A hundred and eighteen years I've sat on the throne, and I am not going to let standards start slipping just because we're in a new era. Millennials haven't made their way to spectral-hood yet. We've got a few years before that headache comes."

The tone of the Midnight Council had been set from then on. Each Baron who held rule over the districts of England gave their reports on activity, detailing everything from disturbances caused by poltergeists, to incidences with paranormal detectives, psychics, and possible-but-improbable discoveries of new conduits.

These reports were often laughed off. The Council was aware new conduits were, indeed, a rare breed. Most of the time when specters believed they had found new conduits, it turned out to be the specter had been gifted with the ability to appear to mortals as balls of light or shadows in photographs and hadn't yet grasped their new abilities.

The topic moved onto the wider reaches of the Empire. In the back rows of the chambers were ambassadors from all partner states of the court. Specters were present from Germany, France, Spain, India, Yemen, Australia, Nigeria, Mauritius, Cyprus, and more.

"The stand now recognizes Amrit Shevade of India."

An Indian man with a slight frame came toward the central podium. He placed some notes on the stand and bowed toward the queen.

"What news from your lands, Amrit?" Queen Victoria asked.

"There is little to tell from our blessed country," Amrit told her. "Your ambassadors are doing a sterling job in ensuring new specters obey our customs. From Mumbai to Bangladesh, there is peace among the majority of the specters, with only a few problems. Much as one would expect from a country of such a size."

"Good to hear it," Queen Victoria told him. "What are these problems?"

Amrit flushed red. He had been hoping she wouldn't ask that question. "It's nothing we cannot control, really. You see, it's the EITC once again. They're still battling the traitors. There's only so long you can fence in unwieldy pirates before they break for the independence of the oceans again."

Victoria frowned. "The East India Trading Company is one of the founding pillars of our modern England, and they are responsible for one of the longest-serving routes for our specters to commute over to your glorious homeland. If they can't handle themselves on the oceans, then we have to remove the problem. If it remains unsolved, then we may have to look elsewhere for our shipments."

"Understood," Amrit conceded. "We do have our forces watching the coasts, and we have bolstered our numbers of specters present on all ships navigating the trade routes. It's just…"

"Just what?" the queen snapped. "Can you, or can you not, control the problem?"

"We can." Amrit nodded. "We will make it so."

One by one, the rest of the ambassadors gave their reports about the affairs in their constituencies. On the whole, there was nothing too unsurprising, although it looked as though the tales of the rebellion in New York had already begun to spread, and small pockets of rebels were appearing in major cities across the globe.

"They're only a small force right now," the French Ambassador, Flora Calvet informed Victoria. "A band of miscreants who call themselves '*Les Guerriers D'été*.'"

Queen Victoria stared at Flora. "In English?"

Flora blushed. "Oh, pardon. 'The Summer Warriors.' They've been caught attempting to recruit members, and have even gone as far as to try to employ poltergeists."

Victoria scoffed. "Peasants. Poltergeists will bow to no one."

"Not true," Flora informed her. "They have had some success."

Victoria shook with rage. "This is why order is needed! Can't you all see? By your lack of action, you have allowed a small problem to flourish and spread. Squash them. Squash them all while they're small. Squash them like the pathetic bugs they are, and then the world will be safe."

The specters gathered around on the benches refused to meet Victoria's eye.

The queen steadied herself, unable to keep the contempt off her face. "Flora. Find a way to disband them before the menace grows. If I hear you have been unsuccessful, then we will have a problem Am I making myself understood?"

Flora nodded and scurried back to her seat.

Richard took her place at the stand and cleared his throat. Before he could say his piece, Victoria interrupted. "Enough out of you, Dick. We know what's coming next. Since we've already broached the subject, what news do you have of Rogue and her merry expedition?"

There were several mutters from the far-off travelers who hadn't yet heard of Rogue's events in New York. A few hands shot in the air, waiting their turn to speak.

"Reports are coming in from all across the city." Nathan Rogers, a specter who looked as though he could easily have just died in court. "It's now becoming an issue of wheedling out who is telling the truth and who is lying. Everyone wants to be the one to report Rogue to you, so now the whole city is seeing her in places where she doesn't exist.

He studied his paper. "Piccadilly, Oxford, Canary Wharf, Clapham, Battersea, Hyde Park, St James's Park, Stratford, Holloway... If we take all of these as gospel, then we're never going to be able to find her."

"I don't care what it takes." Victoria seethed. "Investigate every damn lead we have. It works in her favor if we discount a single one, so I don't care how many specters you need. Find her before she finds a way to get to us!"

Victoria shouted her last words, then sunk into her chair, a sudden headache throbbing in her temple. She massaged her head and took a breath, then looked around the room. "For hundreds of years, my predecessors have ruled the paranormal court, and there has only ever been one true threat to my throne. I took Rogue in and gifted her with the purpose of serving by my side. They say 'keep your friends close and your enemies closer.' Well, this *girl* was as close as any enemy could get. She's the one person who could tear our whole way of life apart, and she's out there running around the city as though she owns the fucking place. I want her. Oh, how I want her in my grasp."

A specter on the benches to her right stood up suddenly and wilted under her gaze. "I thought she was immune to spectral abilities. How do we restrain someone like that?"

A small smirk played on Victoria's face. "No human, conduit, or specter is *immune* to spectral abilities. Everyone has a weakness. Genevieve King's weakness is in the place she has forgotten and left behind in her past."

Every pair of eyes remained fixed on Victoria.

She gave a small chuckle. "Her humanity."

CHAPTER FIFTEEN

Piccadilly Circus, London

George and Melissa walked in silence for some time, enjoying the quiet of the evening under the stars. Now, though, George knew there was something Melissa wanted to say but was struggling to find the words.

She spoke eventually. "Do you ever wonder what it is we're supposed to be doing here? On Earth, I mean. As specters?"

They walked shoulder-to-shoulder, wandering past drunken mortals as the narrow streets gave way to fountains and small greens. "All that action back at the Recess, and you're questioning your existence?" George gave a small laugh. "Your head and mine are in totally different places."

That's not exactly true, is it, Georgie-boy?

Melissa shrugged. "I guess I still have a lot to learn about the spectral world. Every time I think I have it handled, something else crops up. That question back there..." She glanced nervously at George as if he might bite her.

"The one about Victoria and her throne?" George looked up at the sky. "Yeah, it's a question I've often thought about. Are you wondering if we're fighting for the right side?"

He asked the question in as honest a way as possible, but inside he was tense. All it would take was one wrong word to one specter, and it could be the end of life as he knew it.

Melissa looked at him, then turned away. "No."

George shrugged. "Me neither."

They approached the Golden Square, a cute little display of flowerbeds and benches, and walked through the gate.

"This is my stop," Melissa told him. "Thank you for walking back with me."

George smiled. "Sure. After the punch up at the Recess, I figured it wasn't exactly safe to go out here alone."

Melissa chuckled. "Guess people are pretty tense right now, huh?"

George nodded solemnly. He turned to leave.

"George?"

He paused and looked back at her. "Yeah?"

"*Are* we the good guys?" Melissa asked.

George thought for a moment. "I don't think there are good guys and bad guys. Just people who believe in what's right and are willing to act to make the world a better place. And I can tell you without a doubt, Rogue is one of them."

With that, he left.

It took all of five minutes for the Royal Academy of Arts to come into view.

Even at midnight, the building was a sight to behold. With white stonework that proudly fronted the exterior, bold arches, and detailed ornamental work, the building nodded back to the architectural stylings of the Georgian period.

George paused in the street and stared up at the building, enjoying the canvas of stars behind it. The moon was a thin sliver, and it was one of those rare moments where tourists and traffic didn't flood the scene.

A specter waved down to him.

George hadn't intended to visit the building, but he'd found himself walking on autopilot. He waved back, then put his hands in his pockets and took a long breath.

"I can't do it." He thought back to all the countless wrongdoings he'd seen from the queen's men. All the times in life he had fought for good and failed. "I can't do it anymore."

He turned to leave and paused when several specters led by Kershaw appeared in front of him. They blocked his passage and surrounded him in seconds.

Kershaw looked awful. His fight with Clandestiny had left him with a swollen eye, several missing teeth, and bruises across his arms.

"You think this is bad, you should see the other guy," Kershaw croaked. He nodded at Clandestiny who stood behind George. Her own face a reflection of Kershaw's.

"What can I help you with?" George asked as casually as possible. Which, given the situation, wasn't casual. "I was actually about to head home."

"Where's home for you?" Kershaw asked. "Is it with your little gal pal Rogue?"

George raised an eyebrow and laughed. "Oh, come off it. That knock to the head must've been harder than you thought."

"I don't think so," Kershaw growled. "See, your comments earlier got me thinking, and that's something I rarely do these days. You seemed awfully protective of Rogue during our little conversation earlier. Not only that, but you were reported missing from your post earlier, George. AWOL. Where did you go at that time?"

George thought fast. "I told you, I thought I saw Rogue. I left my post to see where she went, but it turned out to be some other mortal."

"A likely story." Clandestiny rolled her eyes.

"We heard your little speech to your lady friend," Kershaw sneered, his mouth growing wide. "Rogue is a good guy, right? Someone wanting to make the world a better place."

George's heart started hammering. "How… What…"

"What's the matter? Cat got your tongue?" Clandestiny howled with laughter and slapped his back so hard he fell to the floor.

When George looked up, he froze, seeing Porter Sykes crouched down beside him.

Every specter within a ten-mile radius of London knew about Porter and Yasmine and their connection with the queen. But what was he doing here?

Porter tilted his head to catch George's eye. "Her Majesty gave us orders to follow up on every minor indiscretion, and every lead across the city concerning Rogue. None of them have yielded such likely paths as yours."

George tried to stand, but he was pushed back down by spectral feet.

He glared at Porter. "You've got nothing on me. I've been nothing but loyal to the crown since my first day as a specter."

"Is that right?" Porter asked as if addressing a fantasy from a five-year-old. "What do you think, cousin? Is he telling the truth?"

A specter materialized beside Porter. A specter with a piranha's grin and a pinstripe suit. He leered and shook his head slowly.

"No? Well, George. Do you hear that? Our American friend here says you're not telling the truth. Do you know how we know?" He paused and waited, although George could tell it was all rhetorical. "Because Rico here has been bequeathed with a rare gift indeed. The ability to remain undetectable and unseen around humans *and* specters."

George could say nothing. He merely growled at the American who had his foot wedged into his back.

"Talk about serendipity," Porter crooned. "Actually, a few of our American friends have made their way to the UK to offer their assistance to the queen in her time of need. Nice, eh? Of course, all of this could be made a lot easier for everyone if we just knew where Rogue was, and where she's been hiding."

Porter snapped his fingers and Rico lifted the pressure off George's back. He leaned in close and whispered, "So why don't you save us all the trouble and tell us where she is?"

George thought for a moment, staring into Porter's eyes. He took a deep breath, then spat in his face.

"Very well." Porter stood and wiped his face. He nodded at the other specters. "As he wishes."

George cried out as the specters closed in and stamped all over his body.

Westminster, London

Jennie could see the outline of Buckingham Palace on the long strip of the Birdcage Walk.

Her heart fluttered as the engine of her car purred. The royal coach was just half a kilometer ahead, and she could see the spectral trail of beefeaters surrounding her.

What if I just jumped out of the car and went for her now? What would happen?

She knew the answer to that question, of course. Lupe had shown Jennie the map littered with crosses to showcase where the guards were watching out. They were in a hot area right now. Hundreds of specters roamed St James' Park to her right, and dozens lined the rooftops. If she so much as showed a single eyelash, they'd be on her like flies around pig shit.

Thank God for tinted windows, Jennie thought.

When the coach was gone from sight, Jennie put her plan into action. Although she had some idea of where all the guards were watching, she wanted to test the limits of her power. What some of her reliables in the tech industry would call a "soft launch."

"Let's go," she told Angus, who looked like the suited man with sunglasses he had masqueraded as before.

"Remember our names?" Angus asked.

Jennie gave him a pointed look. "I'm Mona, and you're Karl. You think this is my first rodeo?"

"You've worked with *Obake* before?" he asked.

"I meant… Actually, never mind. Come on." Jennie stepped out of the car in a glittery cocktail dress, giving off a spectral sheen. She hooked her arm around Angus' and took to the path, walking straight down the Birdcage Walk to the Palace.

They walked in silence, Jennie's eyes glancing in every direction to keep an eye out for suspicious activity. Dozens of specters roamed the Park, pretending to be nothing more than late-night lovers going for a stroll around the green.

"Talk to me," Jennie side-mouthed.

"What?" Angus asked nervously.

"Talk to me," Jennie repeated. " You think it's not going to arouse suspicion if we're just walking silently, tenser than a bull going for a vasectomy?"

"How was your day…sweetie?" Angus managed, with great effort.

"It's a start," Jennie muttered, before saying, "Come on, you don't want me to go into all that. You say how often it bores you. Tell me about you instead."

They passed two specters in Victorian funeral blacks and gave a curt nod.

"Oh, you know I was just kidding," Angus replied. "I love hearing about your day."

Jennie rolled into an improvised rant about how she believed a day in the life of Mona would go.

Angus nodded and gave the right utterances as they roamed

closer to the palace, taking a right into St James's when they saw the number of specters standing guard outside of the palace.

They took to the walking paths, keeping themselves parallel with the long straight road leading to the palace gates as they strolled casually.

A few times, other specters stopped to say quick hellos to the pair, believing them to be old friends. Jennie allowed Angus to take the lead since he was clearly much better informed about the lives of Karl and Mona than she was.

It was when they were within dashing distance of the palace that several things happened in quick succession. The first was a series of laughs from the other side of the green.

Several specters had gathered, hands clutching bellies as they chuckled into the night. Angus pointed at them with sudden alarm, whirling his head to look around before shoving Jennie into a nearby bush.

"Ouch," Jennie complained before seeing what the sudden urgency was.

Two of the specters looked incredibly familiar, and it took Jennie a second to realize why. It was only when the real Karl and Mona turned toward them that she looked down at her cocktail dress and made the connection.

"*Obake!*" Jennie hissed.

"Hey, don't use our name in vain."

"Hush. You're not exactly deities."

"Still…"

Karl and Mona strolled along the path toward Jennie and Angus. Their arms were intertwined, and they wore bright smiles.

"I wonder how long it'll take before they bump into people we've already bumped into," Jennie pondered.

"Never mind that. What the hell are they doing here?" Angus demanded angrily. "They're meant to be on the other side of town."

"How do you know all this?" Jennie asked incredulously.

Angus grinned. "Who do you think put out the call to drag them there?"

Jennie snorted. "Maniacal."

Angus tipped his shoulder. "I do what I can."

The couple came closer. Jennie and Angus retreated further into the shadows of the bushes, not quite realizing, as they fixed their attention on the couple, that they were nearing Birdcage Walk on the other side.

It was only when they heard the sound of struggling, and the occasional groans of a man in distress that they turned, and Jennie's eyes grew wide.

"Oh, Jesus, no," she moaned.

Angus looked at Jennie. "Really? All this spectral-world stuff, and you believe in Jesus?"

But Jennie wasn't listening. Her attention was absorbed by the group of specters man-handling a specter she was all too familiar with.

George struggled in their grasp in an attempt to escape, but the pair holding him gripped him firmly. They trundled toward the palace gates with the man suspended between them and called for the guards to open up.

"Under whose orders?" a surly Beefeater called.

Jennie was reminded of Worthington, and her blood began to boil.

The brute of a man to George's right chuckled. "I think the queen will be interested in a specter withholding information on the whereabouts of Rogue, don't you?"

The Beefeater studied the group with a narrowed eye, then took a step back and gave the command.

The gates swung open, and the specters marched George in.

All Jennie could do was watch with her hand resting on the hilt of the sword at her waist. Her jaw clenched. She could feel the injustice inside of her, gnawing at her like woodworm. The image of George in distress was printed in her mind.

Jennie looked all around, searching for some way to get past the guards and break into the palace. A large part of her wanted nothing more than to storm the gates, whip out the Big Bitch, and put them all out of their misery.

But that wouldn't be smart. There would be too many, even for her. Even if she did manage to break into the queen's chambers, it wouldn't be long before she was surrounded again.

"Think, Jennie. Think…" Jennie had fought against some big groups of specters and won in her time, but she also knew enough about the queen and her men to know it wouldn't be as easy as that this time.

"Is he a friend of yours?" Angus asked with genuine concern.

Jennie brushed away his question with a short reply. "Yes."

She looked all around the palace, noting the line of guards on the roof, in front of the gates, and swamping the surrounding buildings. She turned back to the park and mentally counted all of the specters.

Then she spotted something which made her heart leap—a small something that might be more than she'd ever imagined in this situation.

A female specter appeared from the front of the gates and turned into the park.

Jennie had seen her on many occasions, sitting in on hearings with the queen, and serving as a faithful lapdog for the last few decades, at least.

Yasmine Turner strolled as if she owned the place. Her hands were laced behind her back as she approached each specter to speak for a few seconds before continuing on.

Jennie crept toward her, sticking close to the bushes as Yasmine worked her way closer to their location. They heard her putting extra pressure on the specters to remain vigilant and report even the slightest sighting of anything untoward.

"Okay, I've got a plan, but it might be a bit radical," Jennie told Angus. "It'll involve you playing an obedient servant."

Angus raised an eyebrow. "You've got to be kidding me."

Jennie stared at him straight-faced.

Angus sighed. "Fine."

Jennie closed her eyes and focused on the image of the specter she wanted to imitate. When she opened them again, her outfit had changed, and now she was the spitting image of a specter Yasmine knew very well, indeed.

When Yasmine was close enough to them both that Jennie could see every wrinkle of her nightdress, she hopped out of the bush with a dramatic flourish and stopped in front of her.

"I thought that was you!" Jennie smarmed, doing her best impression of Porter Sykes.

Yasmine placed a hand on her chest. "Porter? What the hell are you doing here? Shouldn't you be over on the north—"

"The north side? Yes, yes, enough of that." Jennie dismissed Yasmine's questions with a wave. "The reports were just hearsay and rumor. Luckily, though, I managed to come across this fellow, who has word on where we can obtain more information on Rogue's whereabouts."

Yasmine gave Jennie a strange look as if trying to decide what was so different about the specter she knew so well. After a few seconds, she seemed to decide everything was okay. "Well, shouldn't we get him to Her Majesty, then? Come on, I'm done with these irksome specters."

"Wait!" Jennie grabbed Yasmine's hand.

Yasmine pulled her hand back. "What?"

Jennie thought fast. "I wanted to investigate his story first, make sure it's all factual. Don't want to waste Her Majesty's time with something that might be a load of old tosh."

"Tosh?" Yasmine folded her arms. "Have you been spending time around Roy Carlton, again?"

Jennie gave an uncertain chuckle. "Yes?"

Yasmine laughed. "You're just like a sponge, you know? He always rubs off on you that way. Come on, show me where to go."

Yasmine and Jennie walked through St James's Park, passing dozens of specters who wilted in their presence along the way.

Jennie felt her heart race when they passed Karl and Mona, momentarily forgetting they had swapped their guise now.

Jennie tried her best to keep small talk to a minimum, and it was only when they walked down a narrow alleyway that Jennie stopped and checked they were, at last, alone.

"Seriously, where are you taking us?" Yasmine chuckled, walking several paces in front of Jennie. "I should've known the bitch would be hiding somewhere in the shadows.

Yasmine turned around, and her face fell.

Jennie had the Big Bitch aimed directly at Yasmine's face. "You say one word, and I'll make sure you don't utter another for days. You got that?"

Yasmine raised her hands and nodded.

Jennie pointed toward the small hatch in the side of the building and ushered Yasmine into the darkness.

CHAPTER SIXTEEN

<u>Westminster, London</u>

Jennie could hear spectral voices carrying through the floor as she approached the hatch leading to the *Obake'* lair.

"Down," she commanded, nudging Yasmine with the Big Bitch.

Yasmine began to pass through the floor. Angus and Jennie followed, aware that if she went faster than they did, she might try to make a run for it.

The talking immediately stopped when they all appeared in the room.

Yasmine stared uneasily around the room. "So, what? You're going to lock me up in a dungeon?"

Jennie prodded the Big Bitch into the back of her head, reminding her of who held the power. "If you're lucky."

Baxter broke free of the specters gathered around. He studied Yasmine from top to tail. "Jennie? Are you going to tell us what's going on?"

"They've got George," Jennie told him.

Carolyn, Baxter, and Lupe started.

"What do you mean, they've got George?" Carolyn asked. "Jennie, what happened out there?"

Jennie explained what she had seen out on the surface, masquerading as other specters along the walk and into the park. She described the volume of specters who stood in their way, finishing with the capture of George.

"Shit," Paige cursed. "Well, he's a goner."

"What do you mean?" Baxter asked.

"Don't you get it? The queen has the ability to exorcise anyone who crosses her. Your friend won't last five minutes in the palace before he's vanquished."

"You're kidding?" Carolyn turned to Jennie. "She can exorcise specters?"

Jennie shrugged. "I've never seen her do it."

Yasmine chipped in. "I have. A snap of her fingers, and you're in the abyss."

Jennie clapped her hands loudly. The sound reverberated around the room like a gunshot, making Yasmine duck and let out a squeal.

"You speak when spoken to," Jennie told her, returning the gun to her head.

"Please, Rogue," Yasmine pled, cautiously glancing over her shoulder and talking slowly. "We've served on the same side for so long. You wouldn't really harm your old friends, would you?"

Jennie tilted her head. "Can't say I was ever very fond of you. Now, one more word, and you won't have a mouth to speak from."

Yasmine shut up.

"So," Baxter ventured, "are you going to tell us who this is?"

"This…" Jennie pulled Yasmine's head back by her hair. "This is one of the sniveling worms who grovel at the queen's feet. Her number three, if I'm not mistaken."

Yasmine held up two fingers.

Jennie smiled. "Cute. You think you were number two? It's obvious your boyfriend has more favor than you."

Yasmine's eyes narrowed.

Jennie ignored the daggers Yasmine stared at her. "Now, here's the plan, as I see it. They've got someone we want free, and we've got someone they want free. If that isn't enough cause for a little parley with the queen, then I don't know what is."

"George won't last the night," Carolyn whined. "She'll kill him at first stroke."

"No, she won't." Jennie fixed Carolyn with a determined stare. "She's not that stupid. George has information on us. She won't destroy him until she finds a way to extract that information. Until he breaks, his life is safe."

"How will she try to extract the information?" Baxter asked with a grimace.

Jennie shook her head slowly. "You really don't want to know."

Yasmine giggled.

Jennie kicked her in the back, and she fell face-first on the packed-dirt floor.

She began to sink into the earth, but Jennie connected with her and pulled her back. When her whole body was back in the room, she aimed the Big Bitch and shot her foot.

Every specter in the room clapped their hands to their ears when Yasmine squealed and writhed, bringing her leg toward her to examine the bloody stump where her foot had just been.

"You bitch!"

Jennie adjusted the aim to Yasmine's face. "You want to say that again?"

For a moment, it looked as though Yasmine was seriously contemplating it. Then she turned away, hissing in pain.

Baxter shook his head but didn't look away. "So, how do we get word of this lady to the palace?"

"That's going to be the difficult part," Jennie admitted. "We're going to need a volunteer, a messenger to gain their attention and draw them out of hiding. Someone to infiltrate the palace and ensure we get to the right people."

She turned to Angus.

His shoulders softened. "How did I know that was coming? Okay, tell me what I need to do."

Buckingham Palace, London

Porter was ecstatic. He roamed through the hallways with a devilish grin on his face.

He had made *some* kind of progress in the hunt for Rogue. He'd captured a weedy little specter he was certain had information on her location.

The specter had been taken to a secure underground cell. When Victoria was finished with her current business, they would fetch the little piece of shit and interrogate him until he either spilled or went to his true death.

How delicious, Porter thought, already imagining the specter's screams. He hardly ever got to play with the torture toys these days, and soon he would be able to break them out and play until the damn fool cracked.

Porter chuckled, moving quickly down the empty hallways until he came to his chambers.

"Yasmine, guess who's got a surprise for…"

He trailed off as he opened the door and found the room empty. He laughed and shook his head, forgetting it would be some time before Yasmine was back. Porter had his side of the city to manage, and Yasmine had hers. Just because he had been successful, it didn't mean she had found anything yet.

He shrugged, then left the room and climbed up a sweeping staircase to the higher reaches of the palace. He passed through attic rooms which had long ago been locked and forgotten, reveling in the musty smell of dust and decay as rats and mice scurried around the room, running from a threat they couldn't see.

As he walked, he thought of Victoria and the situation they were facing. There hadn't been a threat to Victoria or her throne in all of his years as a specter, not really.

Sure, they'd had their fair share of problems from across the world, shapeshifters in Japan, wraiths causing disturbances in Europe, hell, there had even been a few instances of ex-military specters turned *Lawrence of Arabia* in the Middle East.

But there had never been anything as close to home as this.

Rogue was a powerful ally, and an even deadlier foe. Porter had heard enough stories of her capabilities and had seen her return from too many impossible missions to underestimate her. They would need to find her, and they would need to do it faster if they were to minimize the amount of collateral damage she caused in the long run.

Porter passed through a locked door and emerged on the roof of the palace. From here, he could see everything for miles. Specters glowed as tiny dots all around him, looking like a terrestrial reflection of the stars.

He walked up to a sentry guard stationed nearby on the rooftop. The specter still wore his standard-issue camouflage. An SA80 was clutched loosely in his hands as his eyes scanned the perimeter.

Porter looked along the length of the palace, where several dozen ex-forces specters were stationed with a range of weaponry. More SA80s, all had GLOCK 17s, and a few had long-barreled firearms which Porter recognized to be sniper rifles.

"Quiet night?" Porter asked.

"Same as last night, sir," the soldier responded.

Porter nodded and patted the soldier's shoulder. "Be patient. Rogue is coming."

"Affirmative, sir," the soldier replied.

Porter strolled along the roofs, enjoying the peace the deep night brought. In the distance, he could see the London Eye and the Houses of Parliament, places he had once admired in life, but now saw as nothing more than tiresome tourist attractions.

Far off he heard the toll of Big Ben announcing one AM. He turned on his heels and was about to return downstairs, ready to check that Victoria was free, when the soldier called, "Sir?"

He returned to the front of the rooftop and saw the specter approaching down the center of the Birdcage Walk.

"Your lady-friend is home."

Porter shot a look at the soldier, choosing to ignore the small grin pulling at the corner of his mouth.

"At ease, soldier."

Porter met Yasmine as she melted through the doorway. "You're back early." He pulled her to him and planted a kiss firmly on her lips.

She pulled away and straightened her front. "Am I? Well, there was nothing more to do."

Porter raised an eyebrow. "Nothing more to do? You had updates to receive from half the specters of London. You're telling me that only took a couple of hours?"

Yasmine didn't blink. She took a steadying breath. "Yes."

"What's gotten into you?" Porter asked with concern on his face.

Yasmine tucked a lock of hair behind her ear. "It's nothing. I'm just tired, is all. You know what it's like being out there on the streets for hours on end. It makes you tired."

Porter eyed her curiously. "True. Are you sure you're okay?"

"I just need a lie-down." Yasmine smiled. "Come on, you can walk me to my room."

Porter smirked. "You've forgotten where it is?"

Yasmine burst into laughter. "Yeah, right. Good one." She took his hand and pulled him to the right. "Come on."

Porter resisted. "It's this way."

Yasmine blushed. "Just testing you." She kissed him deeply

and stared into his eyes. One of her eyelids twitched. "Come on. You do want me, don't you?"

Porter walked briskly through the palace leading Yasmine by the hand. He ignored the knowing looks cast by the guards roaming the halls. He led Yasmine up the stairs and, when they reached the doorway to her room, pushed her against the wood, his tongue finding its way into her mouth.

She moaned and passed through the wall, leaving Porter to kiss the door.

He entered the room, muttering. "Tease," he accused before advancing on the woman sitting on the bed. "We'll have to make this quick. Her Majesty will soon be calling for a prisoner we've taken who knows the location of Rogue. Nothing gets me hotter than a good interrogation."

He took several steps toward the bed, then froze as the woman he knew as Yasmine began to transform before his eyes.

In the place of the specter he had been about to pounce on was a woman with red hair, round sunglasses, and a leather corset.

Jennie grinned at Porter. "Actually, that's kind of what I needed to speak to you about."

CHAPTER SEVENTEEN

<u>Westminster, London</u>

To give her credit, Yasmine had remained virtually silent the entire time Angus was gone.

Not that she hadn't had a few words to say at seeing another specter turn into an exact copy of her. At first, she had commented that her face couldn't be that bloated. But after confirmation from the others, she'd gone quiet.

Jennie had left the *Obake* in charge of guarding Yasmine, while she and her company awaited Angus' return.

Jennie sat with her back to the wall, a small gold coin in her hand. She played with the coin and rolled it back and forth along her fingers.

"Nice trick," Baxter told her, sitting beside her. Carolyn took the other side, resting her head on Jennie as she snoozed.

"It's not a trick," Jennie replied. "It just takes practice. There's no illusion or mystery; it's just training your muscles."

"I was never able to do anything like that." Baxter held up his hands. "Too big, see?"

"Here." Jennie passed the coin to Baxter. He took it in the flat of his palms and examined it closely. On one side was the head of a person Baxter had never seen in his life, and on the other was an ornate plant decoration. The edges were rough and nicked, and the words were all but faded.

"Trinidad and Tobago. 1799," Jennie told him. "Not in mint condition, but then again, what coinage from that period is?"

"That's before you were born," Baxter marveled.

"You realize time existed before me?" Jennie smirked. "Just because I'm older than you, it doesn't mean *nothing* is older than me."

Baxter frowned. "That's not what I meant…"

"I know what you meant," Jennie retorted playfully. "My parents were hobbyist collectors. They enjoyed museums, they read up on their history, and they even collected a few trinkets along the way. There isn't much of them left in the world, but this coin has lived in my pocket for decades. Sometimes I forget I have it, but when I actually have a moment to sit still, it always comes back to the forefront of my mind."

"You loved your parents dearly," Baxter stated, not a question but a fact.

Jennie smiled sadly. "I did and do."

"I saw the dresser in your bedroom," Baxter commented, placing the coin between the cracks of his knuckles and attempting to roll it to the next finger. "They clearly loved you, too."

Jennie turned to Baxter suddenly. Carolyn snorted in her sleep but did not wake.

Jennie relaxed. "They did. They were the best parents I could have asked for, given the situation. I only wish I could've seen more of them before the whole spectral assassin thing happened."

Baxter dropped the coin, and it clattered on the ground. He struggled to pick it up with his thick fingers.

Jennie chuckled and helped him, picking the coin up with ease.

"This is impossible," Baxter complained, trying once more.

Jennie shook her head. "Nothing is impossible. You and me speaking should be impossible. An entire empire based around a dead monarch should be impossible. Wraiths haunting the grave should be impossible. Yet, here we are."

"You're bitter about those wraiths, aren't you?" he asked.

"You have no idea," Jennie replied.

Baxter tried to flip the coin between his knuckles for another few minutes, dropping the coin with every try. He gave up eventually. "Do you really think George will be okay?"

Jennie chewed her lip. Truthfully, she didn't know what the outcome would be. In her heart, she believed he was far too valuable to be exorcised outright. "I believe so. As long as he doesn't do anything stupid."

"Like what?"

Jennie closed her eyes, trying her best to be patient as Angus got to work. Trying her best not to imagine the worst-case scenario, should George make a simple mistake.

Buckingham Palace, London

There aren't a lot of people who are aware of the hidden vaults beneath the grandiose Buckingham Palace. Originally designed as panic rooms to guard the royal family in the eventuality of a sudden emergency, the impenetrable lead-and-steel lined rooms are linked by a series of interconnecting tunnels.

For those from a spectral background, only a handful was aware that these rooms had since been converted into spectral prisons—empty cubes, guarded by some of the deadliest specters to ever roam the streets of London.

The queen did not want these particular specters to be made public knowledge. These specters had certain abilities and no qualms with doing whatever was necessary to retain their prisoners and keep them incarcerated.

For many of them, the rank of Buckingham Palace prison

guard was nothing more than a perverse form of entertainment for the screw-ups and criminals the world believed it had seen the back of.

George cried out in pain as he was thrown against the cell wall. "You bastards! You can't keep me down here! I'm a respectable specter of the paranormal court! You've got to give me my rights."

His words died in his mouth as he looked up at the giant guard.

The man's shoulders were wider than the doorway. One hand gripped a spiked mace. "You've got no rights down here, sunshine. Down in the dungeon is where *we* play. If you step into our sandbox, you're everyone's fair game."

George picked himself up off the floor and glared at the guard. Behind him stood two more guards, who grinned darkly.

George looked either side of him, then pushed back to pass through the wall a bit at a time.

Something crackled in the air. White-hot pain surged through his body as if electricity had just coursed through him. He was hurled across the room where he hit the brute's stomach.

George fell to the floor and looked around for the source of his pain. He saw one of the guards standing with his palm held flat against the wall.

The guard looked at George as the metal lining the room sparked with jolts of blue electricity. "Try that again, and we're going to stop playing nicely."

"This is nice?" George countered.

The front guard leered. "You have no idea."

"Oh, just tie him up," another guard suggested. "He can't run if he's tied up."

"True," the first guard agreed. "But then that removes temptation, and I want the chance to beat this little fucker to a pulp."

They all chuckled as they passed through the door and exited the room.

George was left alone in the gloom. The prison was lit by a series of small candles running along the corridor, and only a flicker of that light made its way into the cell. He remained seated, aware of the footsteps and passing silhouettes of the monsters outside of his cell.

The time seemed to pass slowly, although there was no way of knowing what the hour was. The darkness enclosed around him. Shouts of protest came from the other cell blocks as the night wore on.

George closed his eyes, drifting into an uneasy sleep. His head filled with dreams and visions of monstrous faces, heavy weapons, and the endless screaming of some horrible thing.

Porter stared intensely at Rogue, his heart beating fast. He was sitting quietly, not caring to admit he was frozen to the spot while Rogue told him she and a group of specters had Yasmine held hostage.

All it would take is for him to hand George back over to them, and to help Jennie get an audience with the queen, and she would go free. "So you want to make a bargain, is that it?"

"I didn't say it was going to be easy," Rogue told him. "But yes. A bargain. Like for like. Brownie points for getting me a short period of time alone with the queen."

Porter's face tightened. "You know I can't do that."

Rogue frowned. "The first bit, the last bit, or both?"

"The last bit," he clarified.

Rogue grinned and leaned her elbows on her knees. "At least that's something. How about we start there and see how we go?"

"You're making a huge mistake," Porter told her softly. "This entire place is surrounded by the finest specters we've got. The lower floors are protected by loyal-to-the-core beefeaters and guards, and the rooftops are lined with soldiers who died in combat and continued to serve. There's no way out of this for you. Even coming here was a mistake."

"A mistake which is worth the risk," Rogue replied firmly.

"And then what?" Porter demanded. "What happens once you talk to Her Majesty? What then? Do you go on your merry way? Do you dissolve the court and rebuild it all from scratch? Every path is anarchy. Every path is destruction."

Rogue leaned forward. "I will not let injustice rule."

A silence passed between them both. Outside the chambers, footsteps echoed as guards patrolled the corridors.

Porter took a long breath. "What if I say no? What then? You'll exorcise Yasmine? Very well. I'll have you killed. You're nothing more than human, remember? You rely on specters to perform your tricks. Without your specters, you are nothing."

Rogue grinned, a twinkle flashing in her eye. "I got this far, didn't I?"

For the first time since Rogue appeared on his bed, Porter realized the mistake he'd made. Of all the powers he had known Rogue to have, she had never been able to transform into other shapes. Only the fabled *Obake* were able to take on the form of other specters.

Not only that, but she had arrived alone. Rogue needed to be accompanied by specters. That was why she was always gifted one from the queen. She was powerless without them.

"Who are you?" Porter asked.

Rogue shimmered and transformed into a perfect replica of Porter. "I'm you, of course."

Porter grew angry. He stood up, fists clenched. "Who are you?"

"I am many people," the specter replied, switching every few seconds into the form of specters they had passed. Once, for a brief second, he even transformed into Queen Victoria. "The only constant is that there is always change."

Porter lunged at the specter and grabbed him by the throat.

They dropped to the floor, wrestling as they rolled around on the antique woven rug.

"Whatever you think you know about me, know this for certain," the specter managed through a constricted windpipe. "We do have Yasmine. I am with Rogue. We will get what we want."

At the mention of Yasmine's name, Porter slowed his attack and released the pressure on the specter's throat. He thought long and hard, taking deep breaths to accommodate for his burst of exertion.

"Fine," he conceded at last. "I'll bring him to you. But you must promise not to touch a hair on her head."

The specter rose to his feet and rubbed his neck. Now he was a perfect replica of Prince Charles. "Absolutely, dear fellow. It's been a pleasure doing business with you. Now, if you would be so kind as to show me a way to get out of here without getting my head blown off by a hundred gunmen, that would be most appreciated."

Alexandria stood in the darkness, enjoying the silence of Elizabeth's chambers.

Royalty lived in the queen's blood. It passed down through time and history, and now it was inside her, in the living monarch of England and all of her children thereafter. Even when abandoned, Alexandria could feel it in the room. Royalty was power, and power was a thing one had to hold close to one's chest.

Even if one had stolen it.

She was the second-biggest threat—Victoria's true living heir. Alexandria had never truly believed Elizabeth would reign for as long as she had. She had been preparing to remove her for years. Yet, while Victoria had taken the mantel of the longest-ruling monarch of the crown, Elizabeth had now surpassed that record by three years.

Which was a blessing and a curse. On the one hand, it was nice to have avoided the sticky situation that had occurred with Elizabeth's father and grandfather, but on the other…

"Oh, how cruel a fate that we must live a life dictated by the rules of others," Alexandria murmured. "How twisted that our lives *should* be superseded by yours. How ill-met that one must take control of the forces of nature to ensure their own survival."

Alexandria imagined how awful it must have been for the queen. The year Victoria had been crowned into specter-dom must have been one of the most overwhelming experiences of her life. To take over the paranormal court during a time of war and instability, and to pull the country and the empire back together with her bare hands…

That would have been a tough cross to bear. The removal of her forebears had made the process easier to consume, and the elimination of those thereafter had finally given the monarch a chance to stabilize the empire and bring the whole deal to rest.

Not without a little help, of course.

Alexandria chuckled. "History is written by the victors. You're welcome, Your Majesty."

Alexandria shifted form, her lithe, slim figure taking on the additional weight of her target, and swept out of the room. The house hadn't changed all that much in the time since she had been living there. Some of the decorations had changed, but for the most part, everything remained as it was.

She met Porter, deep in thought, in the reception room. When she called his name, he started as if awoken from a dream.

"Oh, Victoria."

"Your Highness," Victoria emphasized.

Porter scowled. "There's no one here. Do we need to keep up the façade?"

"It's in your best interests, isn't it?" Alexandria grinned. "I was told you were looking for me?"

"I have a…" Porter hesitated.

"Well?"

"I have a prisoner who might have some information on the whereabouts of Rogue." Though Porter declared it boldly, his hesitation remained.

"Is there a problem?"

Porter shook his head. "No. No problem."

"Good. Lead the way."

CHAPTER EIGHTEEN

<u>Buckingham Palace, London</u>

George huddled in the corner of his little cell and shivered. His body was battered and bruised from the instruments used to try to extract information from him. Even now, lying alone in the dark, camera flashes came to him as swift reminders of the pain he had endured.

But they hadn't broken him.

George held his chin high and rested his head against the wall. He couldn't believe such brutality could exist in the spectral world, yet there it was. The brutes had beaten, they had peeled, they had scratched and threatened to slice, but still, he would not budge.

"Time is the greatest weapon," Victoria had said, standing in the corner with folded arms and a stern expression on her face. "They all wear down with time. Take him back to his cell. We'll try again in a few hours."

George was flooded with relief at those words. Although, he knew he'd soon have to go back to the chamber once more for another round, and even he knew he wouldn't last forever.

"This is the right thing to do," George muttered to himself.

"Rogue is telling the truth. That the queen is doing this to one of her subjects demonstrates it."

A bang on the door. "Quit your whining."

George held his tongue and waited. He waited for the time to pass, hoping Rogue would come and rescue him, but realizing it might not come in time.

Sooner or later, they would break him.

No mountain can last against an endless sea.

George slept.

Westminster, London

Porter walked briskly, glancing in all directions.

Specters had followed him with their eyes, watching with curiosity as he dragged along the whimpering specter they had seen him, not too long ago, drag into Buckingham Palace.

Luckily for Porter, since he stood as the queen's right-hand man, there were few who stood in his way and questioned his behavior.

He raced across Westminster Bridge and toward the meeting destination, arriving just several moments after Big Ben had struck the hour. He reached the back wall of the London Dungeon, and melted through, dragging George with him.

George was ominously silent, but that was perfect for Porter. He didn't want to have to waste any more words on the worthless excuse of a specter.

Following the shapeshifting specter's instructions, Porter made his way into the lower levels, feeling oddly at home amongst the dark, heavy brickwork. Enjoying the sight of the methods of torture which mortals had long ago abandoned as he made his way ever down, down into the forgotten realms.

"You better be worth the risk," Porter muttered as he was about to melt through the final door. "With any luck, this should lead to her actual capture."

George grinned back. "Oh, I know it will."

Jennie was ready when Porter appeared at the doorway. She had Carolyn, Baxter, Feng Mian, and the Order of the *Obake* surrounding her. She raised the Big Bitch and aimed it at Porter.

"Bring him inside," she commanded.

Porter grinned. "Funny. You look much different when you're not being imitated by a specter."

Jennie turned to Angus. "You turned into me?"

He nodded.

Jennie wrinkled her nose. "Ew…"

Porter chuckled. "Before we proceed, I need to see that you're not lying. Show me Yasmine is safe and we can proceed."

Jennie stood firm, her eye trained down the barrel of the gun. "You know I could just blow your head off if I wanted to?"

"I'm sure of that," Porter replied. "I also know I took a big risk in coming here, and you're a woman of honor. Show me your side of the bargain, and we can talk."

He held her gaze, unblinking.

Jennie gave the signal, and several specters dragged a wriggling Yasmine to the front. Without looking, Jennie drew her pistol and aimed it at Yasmine's head. "So much as one sudden movement, and neither of you will be able to speak, kiss, or fuck for a month."

To her surprise, Porter smiled. "How little you think of us! All these years we've known each other, and this is your opinion? At least we're not bending over for Uncle Sam, you traitor."

Baxter took a step forward, anger on his face. Feng Mian stopped him by holding out an arm.

"Hit a sore spot, did I?" Porter crooned. "How about you lower your weapons and we talk this through like real specters?"

"How about you take me to Victoria?" Jennie shot back.

Porter put a hand to his mouth. "Oh, that's right. I forgot you weren't a specter. You must accept my apologies. Only specters should fall under the jurisdiction of Her Majesty. In fact, I'm not sure why visitation rights were ever granted to a *mortal.*"

"You know very well why," Jennie replied, not taking the bait. "Because I get the job done, which is more than can be said about half your order." She thought for a moment, then placed her guns back by her side. "But you're right. Let's talk this through like gentlemen, shall we?"

Porter's face straightened. "Okay, then. Say your piece."

"Very well," Jennie agreed. "The paranormal court is failing."

"Failing!" Yasmine laughed. "Please! It's stronger than ever."

Jennie continued, unperturbed. "Rebel forces are rising across the world. We've seen it firsthand in New York, and I can't believe it took so long for me to see the truth. The world has changed, and the court has struggled to keep up. Her Majesty's Empire has been built on a lie. A system which once worked, and which doesn't anymore. Specters shouldn't be pitted against each other, forced to pick a side to align with. They should be free to roam and choose the afterlife they want. This is a sick and diseased dictatorship, and I've seen first-hand evidence that Queen Victoria will do *anything* to stay in power. Murder her descendants, employ criminals to serve her cause, and even go so far as to manipulate all those around who believe they are serving a better system."

Jennie straightened up and lowered her guns. "The paranormal court is corrupt. If you don't see it by now, then you both must be blinder than I originally thought."

Porter cocked his head, looking as though he was debating her words. The other specters in the room were quiet, each one mulling over everything Jennie had just said. If she could just get through to Porter and Yasmine, if she could just make them see the queen for what she truly was, then maybe they'd have a real shot at getting to her.

Unfortunately, that was not what happened.

Porter clapped his hands slowly. "That was a rousing speech, *Rogue*. You almost brought a tear to my eye." He advanced on her until she raised her gun, and he paused. "You are right about one part, though. It did take you a *long* while to realize what was going on."

Yasmine began to chuckle beside Jennie. She trained her pistol back toward her, a twinkle of uncertainty in her eye.

Jennie thumbed the safety. "Bring George inside. Now."

Porter moved to the doorway and dragged a disheveled-looking George into the room. His suit was askew, and there were shadows across his face.

"Now hand him over," Jennie instructed.

George made a move to run over to Jennie, but Porter held his shoulder firmly. "Before he goes, there is something you should know."

Jennie returned his stare, her mouth a thin line.

"There was never a way you were going to infiltrate the palace," Porter bragged. "No matter what method you tried, someone was always going to outsmart you. I mean, it makes sense when you're surrounded by the most talented specters in the country."

"Jennie, what's he talking about?" Carolyn asked.

Jennie didn't look away from Porter as a brimming smile filled his face.

"I mean, you knew this was a bad idea, didn't you?" Porter goaded. "You knew I would bring an entire force with me, and you'd be trapped by the end of this conversation."

Baxter, Lupe, Feng Mian, and the other specters turned their gaze to the ceiling, wondering if what he was saying was true.

"I told you I would destroy your lover if you played any of your games," Jennie ground out through gritted teeth. "I hold true to my promise. So, tell me. Are you telling the truth, or are you just trying to rattle my cage? Either way, it's going to hurt you. I'm done with your games."

Porter pulled George back toward him and used him as a spectral shield. "You shoot me, you shoot him."

Jennie shrugged. "It'll be worth it."

"Porter?" Yasmine complained. "You haven't seriously gone against your word? We're specters of the crown. Our word is sacred."

"Shut up, Yasmine," Porter snapped. "You don't know what you're messing with."

Yasmine's mouth fell open. "You don't give a shit about me… You'd rather suck up to Her Majesty than ensure I go unharmed!"

Jennie shot the floor near Yasmine, causing her to jump and scream when the sudden movement sent a jolt of pain from her ankle stump.

"Speak now and speak the truth," Jennie commanded. "Have you summoned the Royal Guard to this location. Have you gone against your word?"

Porter allowed a long pause before a single word seeped from his mouth. "Yes."

Jennie exploded with rage. She latched onto George with her spectral power and pulled him toward her, yanking him into her arms as though he were on the other end of a bungee cord.

She hooked an arm around him and held him tightly while she loosed the Big Bitch on Porter.

Yasmine screamed when one of his arms exploded. The other shots grazed his side and took big chunks of flesh from him.

Porter fell to the floor and grabbed at the stump of his arm. Silver slivers of blood leaked from his mouth as he coughed and spluttered.

Jennie stood over him with the gun aimed at his face. "Tell me why I shouldn't just end you now."

Despite everything, Porter began to laugh.

"Think that's funny?" Jennie's eyes grew dark. With her free hand, she drew the sword from its sheath. The silver of the blade shone with its own light.

Porter's face straightened. "A sword?

"Not just any sword," Jenny informed him. "A sword that has the ability to exorcise any specter I cut with it. It took a bit of tracking down, but I was able to get there with a little help from my friends."

Porter stared intently at Jennie. "I call bullshit."

"You want to try it?"

Porter swallowed. "Fine. You wanted the queen. There she is."

A chill ran down Jennie's spine as the specters behind her gasped. The specter she held tight in her arm began to transform. Jennie let go, and standing in the place where George had been a few seconds ago was Queen Victoria.

"Is this some kind of joke?" Jennie asked.

Victoria took a few steps back and shook her head. "How funny that you should ally against me with the order of the *Obake*, yet none of them even recognized one of their own." She smiled at Jennie. "Surprised?"

Jennie let out a whistle. "You could say that."

Victoria raised a hand. "Guards! Seize them!"

Before Jennie could so much as move, specters flooded the room.

Jennie had been in war zones before. She'd been in invasions and raids, and she knew the intensity with which those operations went down.

This took all past situations to a whole new height.

They came in from everywhere, filling the room with the glow of specters. There were shouts from ex-soldiers, ex-cops, everyday specters, coupled with the cries of distress from the *Obake*, Carolyn, Lupe, and Baxter.

Taken by the sudden swarm of specters, Jennie closed her eyes and tried to channel their energy so she could use their power against them. She felt their power flowing through them and imagined the whole swarm exploding outwards, sending specters flying. She strained her muscles, put all of her thought into the action and—

A body knocked into her.

Then another.

Jennie saw special forces entering the room, passing through all of the specters. She realized she was still in human form and that the black uniforms the mortals wore had the initials SIS.

Jennie's heart dropped. The Spectral Investigation Squad were cut-throat humans brought into the circle of spectral intelligence. Founded in 1953, after the great spectral disturbance of Hammersmith, the SIS was an elite force trained to deal with the mortal side of spectral activity.

"Genevieve King, by order of Her Majesty the queen, we order you to freeze."

Jennie was caught. If she became spectral, every surrounding specter grabbed her and held her still. If she went human, the SIS was waiting for her. She fired off several shots and swung her sword, initiating great blazes of painful white light, but the light only served to blind her temporarily.

Jennie was blinking away the afterburn when a sudden shock of pain blazed in her shoulder.

She gasped and grabbed at the place where the SIS captain's bullet had made a deep gash in the top of her shoulder. Blood swelled to the surface, and she dropped her pistol to the floor. "You son of a…"

The captain pointed his gun at her and indicated the troops surrounding her. "I wouldn't be so hasty, sunshine," he told her with a sickening grin. "Sixty years of technological developments, and we've finally managed to duplicate your steampunk-inspired weapon. Want to test us? Go ahead. These bullets will take you down whether you're a human or a specter."

They stared at each other a long moment before Jennie

lowered her shooting arm and spat on the floor. "Congratulations. You've finally caught me. Well done, all. Now, what?"

The SIS officer nodded for one of his subordinates to cuff her. "Now, we hand you over to Her Majesty—"

The room fell into sudden darkness, and a powerful wind whipped up out of nowhere as though a hurricane had suddenly brewed in the very center of the room.

Cries of panic and alarm rang out from everywhere as some unknown presence tore around the room. Guns fired, illuminating a harrowing sight in the strobe light flashes of the muzzles.

A thick, dark fog had entered the room and cloaked them all in its power.

"Your Highness! To the stairs!" Porter's voice called.

Another muzzle flash showed specters fleeing from the room in droves. Another flash and several large, smoky figures hovered in the center of the room.

Jennie looked at the space where the figures hovered in front of her. She reached across the floor for the Big Bitch, squinting against the rushing wind.

She nodded when she felt her fingers close around the grip, then she was carried away from the chaos.

C H A P T E R   N I N E T E E N

<u>Buckingham Palace, London</u>

Disguised as Victoria, Alexandria stormed through Buckingham Palace with Porter and Yasmine following closely.

Her anger was unlike anything she had ever felt before. She'd had Rogue within her grasp. She was moments away from capture or destruction—she didn't care which—and now she was gone.

Not only that, she was gone with the knowledge of what Alexandria truly was, which was an incredibly dangerous thing to have.

Guards moved out of her way without a word, standing to attention as she passed.

Hell hath no fury like a woman scorned.

"Victoria, I—"

Alexandria whirled around and glared at Porter, who supported Yasmine on her one good leg with his one working arm. He sighed as Alexandria melted through a door off the corridor and brought the pair into a quaint little room that was sparsely decorated with paintings and odd bits of furniture. She

177

continued through the room and passed through another door, cocking her ear to ensure they had been left alone.

"What the hell was that?" Victoria shouted the minute they were all in the room. She paced the rug, a dark cloud hanging over her. "What are we supposed to do now?"

Yasmine remained quietly sitting on the floor, clutching her legs and lost in her own thoughts.

Porter, however, shook his head and narrowed his eyes at Victoria. "You have the whole spectral kingdom at your command, and you can't even contain one tiny mortal? Come on, Alexandria. This is a fucking joke."

For the first time, Alexandria's confidence was shaken. She looked questioningly at Porter, struggling to maintain her facade. She looked over her shoulder and, once more satisfied they were indeed all alone, transformed before their eyes.

Victoria disappeared, leaving behind a woman so beautiful it seemed impossible that she was dead. Dark hair flowed down her shoulders, and there was a twinkle in her dark eyes. She wore strange rags over her body, as though life had treated her harder than it should have.

Porter shuffled uncomfortably as Alexandria's eyes bore into his. A terrible darkness emanated from her body.

"What did you two do, hmm?" Alexandria demanded. "Stood there like fucking lepers while Rogue performed her voodoo and escaped from our clutches." She gave a pained howl and grabbed her head. "We had her! We *had* her!"

"Well, we don't, anymore," Porter commiserated. "So, what are we going to do about it?"

"Don't give me that tone," Alexandria snapped. "If it wasn't for you, we wouldn't be in this predicament. 'A sure thing,' you said. 'Rely on her principles,' you said. Well, look where that got us."

Alexandria paced the room, a hand running through her thick locks as she struggled to think. "We have to look at the positives. Rogue and her people still don't know my true identity. Victoria's men and women still have no idea of what the truth is behind the crown."

"That's something at least," Porter admitted.

Alexandria nodded slowly, a finger on her chin. "I'll have to give an address. Let the spectral kingdom know Rogue is out there spreading venom against the crown. Nobody is to believe a word she says. Then we find her. We find her *fast*."

"How?" Yasmine asked, speaking for the first time. She sounded exhausted, her eyes devoid of any real emotion. "She's gone. There's no way of finding her."

"Not necessarily true," Porter countered. "We've still got the prisoner."

Alexandria's eyes lit up. "Oooh! I knew there was a reason I kept you two around."

Porter scowled. "Hey, make no mistake. You wouldn't even be here if it hadn't had been for us. Without us, you would never have been able to work your way into the court. Don't forget who trained you, who taught you everything you needed to know, who found you, and who ensured this plan worked from start to finish."

Alexandria suddenly deflated, a small laugh escaping her lips. She sauntered over to Porter with an exaggerated wiggle in her hips and stopped just inches away from him.

She knew her beauty intoxicated him. She wondered how difficult it had been to kiss her as she took on the visage of Victoria. How hard he'd had to concentrate to remember her true form. All of this while a fat man slobbered on her bed.

She traced a finger down his cheek. "I couldn't thank you enough," she whispered. "For finding me. For removing Victoria. For giving me a second lease of death. How could I ever forget that?"

Porter's eyes widened as she kissed his lips, pulling him close. His eyes darted to Yasmine, who stared at them both open-mouthed.

"Are you serious?" Yasmine shouted, pushing herself awkwardly to a standing position. She hopped over and shoved the pair them apart.

Alexandria gave a coy smirk and stepped back. "What's the problem, darling?"

Yasmine ignored her and hit Porter's chest. "All this time, I thought we were working together so we could direct the paranormal court, and you've been off tonguing her?"

"To be fair," Alexandria remarked, "I'm not always a woman…"

Alexandria cycled through an impressive array of avatars in front of their eyes. One minute she was Alexandria, the next she was a decorated war vet, then a teenage boy, a middle-aged man with a briefcase, a hipster, Justin Timberlake, even a seven-foot-tall basketball player.

"I thought we meant more to each other than that," Yasmine accused Porter, hurt lacing her words. "I got taken as a fucking hostage by the most powerful mortal we've ever known, and you laid my life on the line so you could chance her capture. You risked my fucking *life*." She looked down. " And I only have one leg!"

"You don't have a life anymore, and your leg will grow back, just as my arm will," Porter replied darkly. "You're a specter, remember? And why wouldn't I risk everything when I've worked so hard at ensuring the kingdom is ours for the taking?"

He grabbed her hand in his. "For years, the world has been under the delusion that the real Victoria is on the throne. Our plan has worked elegantly for *decades*. You think I'm going to risk losing all that just because some psychopathic mortal with a God complex thinks she knows better than us?"

Porter released her hand and straightened. "The future of the spectral world is poised on the edge of a knife, and now is the moment which will decide which way the paranormal court falls.

If Rogue is allowed to act… If she so much as nudges us in the wrong direction, this is all over."

Yasmine stared unblinkingly at Porter. When she spoke, her words were barely audible. "You promised we'd do this together."

Porter raised his hands defensively. "I admit that over time, some things changed. But I still love you."

"Pah!" Alexandria exclaimed.

Porter took a deep breath. "Please, Yasmine, understand it from my point of view. We're so close to eliminating the threat, and then we'll be right back where we were. In the driver's seat."

Yasmine's eyes flicked from Porter to Alexandria.

Alexandria waved her hand and gave a sarcastic wink.

Yasmine looked at the floor, then nodded. "You thought you could have it all." She glanced into his eyes. "But you were wrong. I'm out."

She turned and hopped from the room. Heels would have made for a more dramatic exit, but she was down a foot.

The sound of Porter's desperate pleas faded with the slamming of the door.

Kensington, London

The world dissolved around them. For several long minutes, all Jennie was aware of was the black smog and a rushing whoosh as though she were speeding through a tunnel. Her feet didn't touch the floor, and she allowed herself to be taken in that moment of immaterialism.

There were few moments in Jennie's life where she felt she could let go. For years she searched for the answer to inner peace, and she had made great waves in understanding the fundamentals of meditation and learning to harness her own mind.

But to be totally free—that was a rare euphoria.

It was out of her hands now. As the smoke had emerged,

Jennie searched for some kind of energy to latch onto and found nothing. Nothing more than a mystic air that cocooned them and shrouded them in its warmth. Maybe they were traveling through London. Maybe they were being taken through a separate dimension.

It didn't matter. All that mattered was the calm bathing them all.

Momentary bliss is something worth savoring, Jennie thought, remembering the words of her former instructor. *Take the moments and stretch them, immerse yourself in them. When they come, it is a blessing. Good things happen to those who listen to the universe.*

Was this the universe responding to Jennie now? Jennie had experienced various kinds of phenomena people would likely call magic, but could this be a new kind? Some physical manifestation of a universe that had gifted her powers and now protected her in her time of need?

Somehow Jennie didn't think so. She had an inkling, but it wouldn't be until they once again hit solid ground that she would know for sure.

When the end did come, it was with a suddenness that unsettled the group. Jennie's feet connected with the earth and she folded to her knees, using her hands to support her landing.

Some of the others were not so graceful. Baxter collapsed onto his back, Carolyn rolled as though she'd just jumped down a hill, Lupe landed on his ass and hissed in pain. Angus, Paige, and the other *Obake* toppled on top of each other in an ungraceful pile.

The only other specter to land gracefully was Feng Mian, who knelt stoically on the floor, having allowed his knees to take the impact. He placed his hands on the earth and bowed, sharing a silent prayer of thanks.

Carolyn moaned. "What the hell just happened?"

"Where are we?" Lupe grunted, massaging his lower back with a hand.

One by one, the specters pulled themselves to their feet and looked around their surroundings.

They were in a large chamber with walls, ceiling, and floors made of packed dirt. Roots lined the walls like veins, and there were several candles along the edges of the room, flickering in a ghostly light.

Baxter turned to Jennie. "No…"

Jennie grinned. "I guess so."

"What? What is it?" Carolyn asked, then screamed as smoke began to appear in the center of the room, followed by the sudden appearance of some greater coalescing, flapping wings of smoke like an enormous bird.

The smoke took solid shape and revealed the wraith who now hovered and stared at Jennie.

"You've changed your mind?" Jennie asked.

The wraith stared at her.

"Changed their minds?" Carolyn grabbed Baxter's arm with alarm on her face. "What's she talking about? What is that?"

Jennie moved closer to the wraith. She spoke slowly, enunciating each syllable. "Have. You. Changed. Your. Mind?"

The wraith gave an almost imperceptible nod.

Jennie's whole body relaxed as if the weight of everything had rolled off of her. "Thank you. You don't know what this will mean for us."

The wraith now spoke in a voice devoid of emotion and tone, the sound like air whistling down an empty tunnel. "Our line is tarnished. A threat among our kind is in play. You must protect what is ours and restore our legacy."

Jennie turned to the others and spoke behind her hand. "Talk about a tall order. Can you believe this guy?"

What few chuckles there were soon dissipated. The wraith waved its arm and a scroll appeared. It was covered in writing, with space at the bottom to sign.

"Name your conditions," Jennie told him.

The wraith answered without hesitation. "Eternal peace."

Jennie considered this, then took the spectral quill offered by the wraith and scrawled at the bottom. "So be it."

The moment the parchment was signed, the wraith vanished from the room in a puff of smoke and left Jennie, Lupe, and the specters behind.

A long silence followed since no one was quite sure what to say, until Carolyn broke the quiet. "Will somebody please tell us what the fuck is going on?"

CHAPTER TWENTY

<u>Kensington, London</u>

They sat in the chamber for a long while, deep in discussion about everything that had occurred that night.

"I always knew something wasn't quite right," Jennie declared. "There was always something off about the three of them together, but I thought it was more of a love triangle situation. I would never have guessed Queen Victoria had been replaced by an *Obake*."

"You had zero idea that Victoria was an *Obake*?" Paige asked. "Like, none?"

Jennie shook her head. "Of course not. How do you detect an *Obake*? None of you worked it out in the dungeons, did you?"

Paige looked at the floor.

Jennie frowned as she thought back. "Porter and Yasmine have been at Victoria's side for as long as I can remember. Since way back before the Beatles rose to fame—who, incidentally, are not the best kissers."

"Excuse me?" Baxter laughed.

"Not now, Bax. They were brought to her…hmm, it must have been around 1936, when George V would have been due to take the crown—not that anyone remembers that, of course. All that business would have been swept under the carpet.

"Once they took her side, things got a bit more turbulent. At first, I thought Victoria had just been blessed with a new lease on life, but looking back, her mannerisms did alter."

Carolyn shuffled on the floor. "How do you mean?"

"Victoria was never the most active ruler," Jennie explained. "She was famed for being somewhat...comfortable in her ways." A ripple of laughs went around the room. "So, to see her roaming enthusiastically around the palace, barking orders, and laughing with the staff was a bit of an adjustment."

"Are you saying that was when the *Obake* came in and took Victoria's place?" Baxter asked. "Because if that's the case, what the hell have they done with the real queen? Surely someone knows what happened to her?"

Jennie mulled this over while the other specters waited expectantly. To them, it was like storytime at Grandpa's, only with real stakes that would affect the whole spectral empire.

"That's the question," Jennie mused. "It all must have happened around the same time, which means Victoria must be hidden somewhere in the palace. They must have her captive somewhere." Jennie gasped and put a hand to her head, "Which would go toward backing up my theory about the oaths."

"What?" Lupe exclaimed. "How?"

Carolyn answered for her. "Because for over sixty years, people have been obeying the command of an imposter, not the word of the true queen. Jennie, this is huge!"

"Bigger than we first thought," Feng Mian commented quietly. "The *Obake* are an ancient order. For one of them to infiltrate the palace is sacrilege."

The specters began to murmur among themselves. Paige and Angus looked pained as they tried to understand how one of their own could have been existing under the radar in London for so long.

"So, where do the wraiths come into it all?" Carolyn asked, earning the group's quiet once more.

Jennie gave a small smile. "The wraiths are an ancient form of specter, created when a family line is bound together in the hollows of the ground. Blood honors blood, and with the gift of remaining with family comes the curse of the form you have seen before you."

Baxter took over. "These wraiths were the reason Jennie and me split from you guys several days ago. We asked for their assistance in breaking into the palace, and they refused to help."

"Why do we need them?" Lupe asked. "If they're bound by blood to remain here, why would they help us?"

"Many reasons," Jennie replied cryptically. "The primary reason being that they bear the gift of invisibility, and that's something we can certainly make use of, isn't it?"

"I'll say," Carolyn uttered.

"What do you think they'll do now?" Angus asked. "The crown, that is. They've seen us. They know we're here. Their security is going to be tighter than ever—as if it wasn't tight enough already."

"I've been thinking about this," Jennie replied. "But I don't like the answer I'm about to give. They're going to go for George, harder and more viciously than ever. We've got to pull all our talents together to ensure we can make this work. When it does, we will finally have some answers and be on track for setting the world straight again."

"What do you think those answers are?" Carolyn asked. "What else can we possibly unveil?"

Jennie lifted her hands. "I don't know the answers. What I do know is that whatever dirt is down there, it needs to be dug up. Maybe the queen hasn't been behind the conspiracy, but somewhere along the way, something has gone wrong with the court. It's on us to fix that."

The specters nodded in unison.

"What if George cracks?" Baxter asked with concern. "It's not like they know anything about where we are now. They don't know about the wraiths, or what we're planning to do next."

"No, they don't," Jennie replied flatly. "But they might extract the location of my hideout. If that happens, I'm going to be extremely pissed if they break my stuff."

"More pissed than you already are?" Carolyn asked.

Jennie smirked. "Sweetie, you haven't *seen* me pissed yet.

When everyone had finalized their plans, a single wraith led them back through the crypt and out into the abandoned patch of the graveyard.

The sun was beginning to rise. A burning orange and pink stained the sky. A few stars remained behind, reluctant to join their brothers and sisters in sleep.

The wraiths were waiting for them outside the mausoleum entrance. A handful of them, led by Canute, the largest of their order, hovered above the dew-kissed grass.

"We're ready," Jennie told him.

Canute breathed deeply, the sound a rattle in his throat. "You are certain this is your path?"

Jennie nodded. "Yes. This is also your path."

Canute gave a slight nod, and the next thing they knew, the wraiths encircled them all.

"Hold on to your balls," Jennie muttered.

The wraiths became immaterial and encircled them, and the wind began whipping at them as they were pulled rapidly into a darkness that resolved into the realm of smoke.

The journey didn't seem so long now that Jennie was prepared for the method of travel. When they touched solid ground again, they found themselves in a large attic filled with old treasures and covered in dust and cobwebs.

"Where did they bring us?" Baxter asked, looking around the space at a variety of cardboard boxes stuffed with photo albums, Christmas decorations, and bags filled with old clothes.

"You can ask them yourself, you know," Jennie told her.

Carolyn shook as she approached the nearest wraith. Her voice trembled. "Ex-excuse me?"

The wraith turned to face her, revealing the empty darkness under the hood of its cloak. It turned toward the far wall and pointed a long slender finger.

Carolyn crossed over to the angled window the wraith indicated, which was so neglected that a layer of grime obscured the view. In the parts she could see through, Carolyn saw the London rooftops. The sun had now begun its ascent and the light stung her eyes, but even as she blinked and raised a hand, she could see Buckingham Palace in the near distance.

Not only that, she could see hundreds of specters spread out across the rooftops.

She ducked out of sight.

"What is it?" Jennie asked, moving to the window.

"Stay down," Carolyn urged. "They're everywhere. They've brought us right into the heart of everything. For all we know, there are specters a few meters above us."

They looked at the ceiling, each specter now lowering their voice.

Jennie turned to Canute. "Why have you brought us here?"

The wraith took another rasping breath. "The ancients know the old ways. Forgotten ways. The secrets of your destination. Those who wish to remain here to watch the events unfold, this is as safe a place as any within viewing distance."

"You heard the wraith," Jennie whispered to the room of specters. "Speak now, or forever hold your peace."

Several of the *Obake* sheepishly took a seat.

Paige and Angus growled. "No one stays behind," Angus ordered. "We're in this together."

There were some murmurs and grumbles, but the specters rose to their feet.

"Good," Canute intoned. "Follow me."

Jennie accompanied Lupe while they followed Canute and his wraith companions descent from the attic and navigated through the old, abandoned house. Lupe was aware that he was the only one who physically needed to use doors. Every now and then, Jennie thought she could hear someone moving around the house, but it had to be her imagination.

They reached a pantry on the bottom floor of the four-story building and went inside.

Canute pointed to the floor. "Here."

"What am I looking at?" Jennie asked. She scraped the floor with her foot and revealed the outline of a small hatch beneath a thick layer of dirt and dust.

"Does everyone in this city have a hidden underground tunnel?" Baxter asked incredulously. "In New York, the only things below the ground are specters, the subway, and dead bodies."

"Oh, the cultural dissonance." Jennie grinned, searching for something to lever the hatch open. The square was concrete with no visible handle.

"Here," Lupe called, finding a crowbar hanging on the wall and handing it to Jennie.

She jammed the edge into the ground and pulled until the hatch popped open with a reluctant hiss. Stale air that had been trapped for an unknown number of years filtered into the pantry.

"Jesus!" Baxter put a hand over his nose and mouth. "That's fresh."

They jumped down into the tunnel, Jennie and Lupe falling a full ten-feet before they hit the ground. Jennie drew a flashlight and shone it down the tunnels that stretched off in both directions.

"Lead the way," she muttered to Canute, as he and the wraiths swept ahead, swallowing nearly all of the light that shone from her torch.

Despite their age, the tunnels were relatively straight and had stayed in good condition. Aside from a few minor collapses along their way, which the wraiths directed them around, the journey was smooth. The only thing that changed was the atmosphere as they grew closer, a nervous tension surrounding them with every step they took.

The wraiths pulled to an abrupt stop directly below a hatch in the ceiling. A rusted ladder was the only access.

Jennie tested the metal with her bare hands. "There's no way this will take our weight," she told Lupe. "Looks like you might be stuck in the tunnel, my friend."

Lupe looked more relieved than annoyed, but he still protested. "There has to be another way."

Jennie shrugged and turned to Baxter. "Bax, will you do the honors?"

Baxter nodded, then used the ladder to lever himself upward. The metal didn't even creak. When he neared the top, he cautiously poked his head through the hatch and looked around.

After a few seconds, he pulled his head back into the tunnel and gave Jennie a thumbs up. "I think we're good. It's just a dark room. Another pantry, I think. Smells like stale cheese and wine."

"Okay." Jennie turned her attention to the specters. "Who's next?"

One by one, the specters climbed into the room. The wraiths waited patiently below until at last it was Jennie's and Lupe's turn. No one in their right mind would believe Jennie and her specters would have been able to find a way into the palace, let alone have traveled there so soon after the confrontation at the dungeons.

"Wait there," Jennie told Lupe, latching onto Carolyn in front of her and turning spectral.

"What else is there *to* do?" Lupe asked, looking nervously at the wraiths.

Jennie pulled herself into the room, immediately agreeing with Baxter's deduction that the room stank of wine and cheese. Not good cheese, either. This smelled like it had been placed in storage and long forgotten.

Unless someone upstairs is a connoisseur of cheeses. Maybe there's some super-stinky gorgonzola I'm unaware of?

Levering herself into the room, Jennie scanned the shelves and looked for something of use. There was plastic packaging, long lengths of twine, and a barrel of used corks to plug the top of wine bottles. Nothing sprang out as something that could be used to haul someone through a hole in the floor.

"What about this?" Baxter asked, pointing to a set of empty shelves. Wooden ledges rested along four metal poles.

"A bit big to use as a ladder. It wouldn't fit through the holes."

"Not the shelves," Baxter clarified. 'The poles."

"That could work." Jennie set to dismantling the shelves quietly. Although she was almost sure they were far from the prying eyes and ears of specters, she wasn't going to risk being caught.

When she'd worked a pole free, she levered open the hatch and lowered it down.

Lupe grabbed the pole with trembling, clammy hands, clearly not dealing well with being left alone with the wraiths. He let out a few strange noises as he fought for purchase.

After a few failed attempts, he wiped his hands on his clothes, jumped in the air, and grabbed the pole with all of his strength.

"Quickly!" Jennie allowed the specters to pull her backward and lift Lupe from the tunnel.

He made it halfway before his hands slipped. He flailed and clutched onto the edge of the hatch with his fingertips, his legs dangling below him, and whispered for help.

Jennie grabbed him by the armpits, hooked her arms, and

raised him higher. Her strength was impressive, and soon he was panting on the floor.

"Thanks," he told her gratefully.

Jennie pressed her ear against the door where she could just make out the sound of specters talking, then put a finger to her lips. "We have company."

CHAPTER TWENTY-ONE

<u>Buckingham Palace, London</u>

The specters did not sound happy.

Jennie considered poking her head through the door to hear the conversation better, then thought better of it when the wraiths appeared through the floor and joined them in the room.

"Canute," she purred. "It's showtime."

Carolyn whispered. "Why does she always say that?"

Baxter leaned closer. "Theater obsession."

Carolyn nodded her understanding.

Canute ushered a wraith forward with a silent signal, and Jennie focused on connecting with his energy. The wraiths had a different frequency than typical specters, and Jennie had to spend a few seconds homing in on the dark chill that emanated from him.

When she had locked on and was drawing on the wraith's energy, she took a breath and stepped through the wall.

Jennie was startled for a moment by two hulking specters involved in an angry conversation who were walking directly toward her. She panicked and was reaching for her weapon when she realized they couldn't see her.

Jennie dropped her hand as they walked through her.

Specters upon specters upon specters. It's like Inception *for ghosts.*

Sallow bulbs lit the long, straight tunnel. Jennie followed the specters a short distance along the bare concrete, then stopped when one shoved the other a little too hard and sent him into the wall.

The specter who had been pushed recovered and shoved the other specter. They glared at each other, and it looked like something more was going to happen until one of them said,

"Enough of this shit. We need to stick together, not push each other apart. We've got a job to do, and Her Majesty won't be happy if we fail."

The other one hesitated before adding, "Fine. Let's just get the fucking prisoner and deliver him. When did we become glorified delivery boys?"

The other specter chuckled. "Around the time we died, I think."

Jennie ducked back into the room, her heart racing.

"Where are we?" Baxter asked. "Who was out there?"

"Bhoots," Jennie told him.

The specters gasped.

"What are Bhoots?" Lupe asked, jumping in before Carolyn could.

Jennie thought about the best way to describe them. "Not specters you want to encounter. They're murderers who refused a priest before being executed. Thugs who abused their mortality and were forced into the afterlife with no one to bless their passing."

"So they're just specters?" Carolyn asked. "Pissed-off specters?"

Baxter answered, "I'm afraid not. When the truly evil have no remorse, the spectral conversion can take a funny turn. Bhoots have greater strength and different abilities than regular specters. I've never met one before, but I've heard of a group around New York who, luckily, keep to themselves."

"The bitch is recruiting everyone she can, isn't she?" Carolyn seethed.

"I think they know where George is," Jennie informed the group. "They were talking about a prisoner they're delivering to someone. It's got to be him."

"Wait, where is this prison?" Angus asked. "I've studied London history for years. I've seen floorplans. There was never any mention of a prison in the palace."

"Yeah, well, like a lot of what we're discovering, this place is full of secrets." Jennie narrowed her eyes. "Look, wherever the hell we are, we need to put the plan into action, okay? It's time to split up. I'll go with Canute and the wraiths, and you lot cause a disruption and find a way to free George."

There was a general murmur of agreement.

Jennie turned back to the wall and prepared to turn invisible once more.

That'll have to do.

There was nothing left for it. Everything was beginning to fall apart, and it was on Porter to fix it all once again.

He ground his teeth as he marched through Buckingham Palace. His route took him down the hidden passageway and into the cells below. Rogue was threatening to take everything from him, and he just couldn't allow it. He unconsciously rubbed a hand over the place where his arm was beginning to grow back.

Two Bhoots barred the entrance to the cells. He barged between them, waving their aggressive protests away, and stormed down the corridor toward the prisoner's cell.

How could this have happened? Only a few months ago, everything had been in order. Now, he had pissed off two women

—three, if he included Rogue—and there was every chance the empire would collapse if he didn't sort things out and fast.

It would all come down to the shit-eating prisoner—the fool who refused to spill his secrets.

Not for much longer, bucko. It's my turn to take you to the torture chamber, and this time I don't think things will be so nice for you.

George's cell came into view.

"Ready for round two?" The guard grunted with excitement. "Do I get to watch this time?"

"Fuck off, you sadistic clown," Porter snapped. "Bring the prisoner to chamber seventeen. Feel free to soften him up a bit along the way."

Jennie sneaked through the hallways on her tiptoes, accompanied by Canute's wraiths. Even though she was invisible, she wasn't sure if she could be heard and thought it best to place extra caution where she could.

The place was a labyrinth of long hallways. Several times she passed through Bhoots roaming the halls. Others were guarding the doors of rooms where the inmates were being tortured. Jennie cringed every time she heard someone screaming, praying the next scream she heard wouldn't be George's.

When she reached an intersection, she paused and tucked herself tight against the wall. Porter strolled toward her with a determined expression on his face. Behind him were two Bhoots hefting George by the arms, while his legs dragged on the floor.

Jennie made to go to him but hesitated at an icy hand take her shoulder.

"You must remain focused," Canute reminded her.

Jennie reluctantly nodded, knowing her specters were on George's trail. With any luck, he'd soon be free. Before she continued up the corridor, she latched onto the Bhoots just enough to pull their energy to confuse them.

She dashed in the direction Porter had come without looking back.

Eventually, she found the stairwell leading to the main rooms of the palace. She passed effortlessly through the guards at the doors, eliciting nothing but a slight shudder as she went through them.

One guard turned to the other. "You feel that, Pen?"

"Man up," Pen replied. "You're imagining things."

Jennie emerged through the floor of the palace, and found herself somewhere she was more than familiar with.

The palace had been home to Jennie at a time when she'd had nowhere else to go. In her early years of working with the paranormal court, she had taken a room in the palace at the command of Victoria. It was only as time went by and Jennie realized she needed to have some kind of separation from her work that she had constructed the hideaway beneath the Savoy and made that her permanent home.

Now the halls felt strange. It had only been a few weeks since she was last here, and already everything felt different. Her memories of this place were tarnished, brushed with the new reality she had uncovered.

Jennie got her bearings, made a mental map of where she was going to search, and got to work.

This is never going to work.

Lupe, Carolyn, Feng Mian, and Baxter walked in the center of the *Obake*.

Although, they didn't look like *Obake*. They towered around them all, their Bhoots disguises complete with thuggish walks and tree-trunk arms. The specters did a stellar job of imitating the prison guards, but Lupe had little faith that the real Bhoots would fall for their ruse.

They came around a corner and were met by two Bhoots standing guard outside a cell where it sounded like someone was crying. The dull thuds of punches and kicks could be heard from within.

"Who are you?" one asked, moving to block their path.

"New blood," one of the *Obake* grunted. "Got some prisoners for the queen. Been instructed to bring them down to seventeen."

The guard arched an eyebrow. "Seventeen is occupied."

"Did you mean fifteen?" the other guard asked.

The *Obake* shook his head. "Yeah. Right. Fifteen, that sounds about right."

The guard who blocked their path gave them a curious look, then stepped away. As Lupe and the others passed, he growled and clenched his fists.

Lupe looked at the floor to avoid their eyes.

Along the way, there were several more encounters of the same ilk. Only once did it look like they were about to be foiled when one of the Bhoots put up more resistance than the others. On that occasion, Carolyn acted by trying to make a run for it, after which one of the *Obake* chased her and brought her to the ground and laid into her with a couple of pre-rehearsed kicks and punches to ensure the whole facade looked real.

"Let us through *now*," the *Obake* told the Bhoots. "Before a prisoner escapes and I have to tell Her Majesty it was you what let her go."

The Bhoot cursed and reluctantly stepped out of their way, muttering, "Yeah, like anyone could escape this prison."

When they reached a quiet stretch of corridor, Lupe asked Baxter how they were going to be able to find George by just wandering around. Surely, they were going to look even more suspicious, just casually strolling the halls?

"That's a risk we have to take," Baxter told him. "Luckily, it looks like there's a chronological system here, look."

He pointed to the numbers on the cells, crudely drawn in spray paint. They had reached number twelve, and number fifteen was up ahead.

"Shit," Baxter cursed.

The doors to number fifteen weren't guarded since there was no prisoner inside. When they reached the doorway, they all stopped, the *Obake* encircling the others enough to mask them.

"What the hell do we do now?" Carolyn asked, just as a screaming came down the corridor. It was slightly muffled, but it was clearly the sound of someone in pain.

The specters looked at each other with concern while the *Obake* checked the corridors to make sure the coast was clear.

"Stay here," Angus told them.

He returned shortly later with a worrisome face. "There's a chamber just around the corner and up a ways. Is your friend a former politician?"

"How did you know that?" Baxter asked.

"Because even under torture, he's lying through his teeth." The *Obake* tried to hide his smile, clearly proud of his joke.

"Is that supposed to be funny?" Carolyn asked.

"There's no time for that. Take us to him," Baxter demanded.

They were about to set off again when two Bhoots rounded the corner behind them.

"Hey. You haven't locked them up yet? What's the hold-up?"

Angus stepped forward. "Tuffnell lost the keys again, didn't he? Fucking idiot would lose his head if it weren't screwed on."

The Bhoot paused a short way in front of them. His face was pained. "We don't need keys. We're spec—"

Angus threw the first punch, and the *Obake* peeled away from the group to take on the other Bhoot. Taken off-guard, the Bhoot guard stumbled backward, shaking his head to try to regain his composure. The second Bhoot, on the other hand, charged at them, growling.

"Go," Paige urged—at least, they thought it was Paige—pushing Lupe and the others back.

Baxter's face set. "Come on. She's right, we've got to go."

Baxter, Lupe, Carolyn, and Feng Mian turned and fled down the corridor, with a handful of *Obake* beside them. They turned right and ran toward the sounds of screaming, pausing outside a door where the source of the noise was the strongest.

"Here goes nothing," Baxter ventured, prepping himself mentally to pass through the door and attack the torturer.

An *Obake* hand held him back. "Wait. Let us. This could be fun."

C H A P T E R   T W E N T Y - T W O

Buckingham Palace, London

The noises made by a man in pain filled Porter with an electric feeling he couldn't describe.

He had never seen himself as a sadistic man in life, but in death, there was something deliciously satisfying about inflicting a pain he knew would heal. Cut off a specter's limb, and a new one will grow back in time. Peel off a toenail or cut along the flesh, and all would be well again in a few days—a few weeks, tops.

All that would be left behind is the memory of a specter pushed to their limits.

"Tell me what you know!" Porter barked at the prisoner on the table. A man bound by coils of spectral rope and covered in bruises. The Bhoots were the perfect allies for this sort of activity, and they reveled in it almost as much as Porter did.

George's head rolled on the table as if it wasn't connected to his body. His eyes were puffy slits. "I...told you," he panted. "She's...right...behind you...*fucker.*"

He gave a painful laugh, spluttering and coughing as he did.

Porter shook with rage and marched to the side of the room.

Over the years, the paranormal court had acquired a variety of spectral instruments that had accompanied mortals into their deaths. Specters had whatever they had on them when they died, and there had been more than one doctor slip the mortal coil while tending to their patients.

Porter now picked up a surgeon's scalpel with his remaining hand and walked back to the table. He held the blade in front of George's face. "Do you know what this is?" he asked menacingly.

"The stick you keep up your ass?" George asked, matching Porter's stare.

Porter grinned without humor. "It's your undoing. Figuratively and literally. Now, if you refuse to cooperate, I'm going to be forced to make one tiny cut after another in vertical lines down your body until you do. By the time I'm finished, you'll look like the collection bin of a crooked lawyer's shredder. Here's an advanced warning to you. My patience is all gone. Tell me what I need to know, and you will be set free."

"You think I haven't been around politics long enough to smell bullshit?" George argued. "I give you what you want, you'll exorcise me before I've even finished my sentence."

Porter debated this. "That's definitely a possibility."

George lifted his chin. "I'll take the alternative—suffering with honor."

"Honor!" Porter laughed. "What honor is there in suffering for a delinquent with a warped view of life? You're protecting no one; you're just risking the collapse of the age-old order that has kept the spectral world at peace for as long as anyone can remember."

"That's what you rely on, isn't it?" George choked. "People forgetting."

Porter watched him for a few moments, then sighed. "Very well. You've made your bed, so you can lie in it."

Porter took his time dragging the blade through George's flesh, reveling in the pained yelps of the prisoner. The first cut went into the shoulder while the Bhoots held him still and allowed Porter to do his work.

He made it to George's toes, then examined his work. "Not exactly straight—"

"Like you?" George panted.

Porter seethed. "Good thing I'm not trying to win any prizes, eh? I wonder how this will work on your face." He returned to the top of George's body and held the knife an inch from his eye. "Could be a fun place to start."

He was about to plunge the knife into George's eyeball when a movement caught his attention. He turned to the door and jumped when he saw Alexandria standing there, disguised as Queen Victoria.

He side-eyed the guards. "Alex— I mean, Your Majesty. To what do I owe this pleasure?"

"Unhand that man," Victoria ordered. Though her voice was hers, there was something off about the way she said the words. Porter had spent enough time around Alexandria to know she had the Queen Victoria impression nailed.

"Is something the matter?" Porter inquired. "We're in the middle of extracting information from the prisoner."

Victoria took a few uneasy steps forward, then leaned over the table and seemed to struggle with the sight of the bruised and battered specter. "I can see that," she told Porter. "Unhand him. New information has come to light, and we must have him kept in one piece. You can have him back once everything is settled, I assure you."

Porter looked quizzically at Alexandria, questions bubbling in his head. Was this her? Had the pressure of the last few days finally gotten to her?

His eyes widened as he had a sudden flashback to the image of Yasmine sitting on his bed and morphing into Rogue. He ordered the guards to grab her.

But this Victoria lookalike was fast. She lunged at him, her thick hand grabbing his wrist and wrestling him to the floor. The knife shone between them, glinting in the flickering flames of the candles. Porter struggled with only one arm to fight with, but he was strong and held fast.

"Well, don't just stand there, morons. Do something!" Porter shouted.

The Bhoots stood stupidly for a few moments, staring between the pair on the floor. They had never seen Victoria this way, and the last thing they wanted to do was upset the queen by interfering without her permission.

That was reinforced when Victoria shouted, "Stand down!"

"No, you fucking idiots." Porter grunted, doing whatever he could to free the blade. "She's an imposter. A fake. Get her off me!"

"I don't know, sir," the Bhoot disagreed. "She looks pretty real to me."

Porter grimaced as he mustered his strength. He rolled back to try to gain the advantage. Whoever this bitch was, she was strong. He found himself filling with a real sense of panic. Where was Yasmine when he needed her?

Off somewhere in the wild. Good luck to bad rubbish.

Porter roared with the effort of his exertion as he managed to make his way on top of Victoria—which was tough, considering how rotund her stomach was. He straddled her and gave a sharp tug, freeing the knife and plunging the blade into his attacker's chest.

"Your Highness!" the Bhoots shouted, a sudden panic on their faces at the sight of the queen being stabbed.

But as they raced to get involved Victoria vanished in front of their eyes, transforming into a perfect replica of one of the guards.

"What the..." the Bhoot's anvil-sized hand dropped Porter's collar.

"Now!" the *Obake* shouted.

Porter turned in dismay as several specters and a scarred mortal ran into the room.

Baxter was the first to appear, his massive frame almost a match for their opponents.

The two guards quickly rose to their feet, glee spreading across their formerly stony faces.

"Finally, a chance for some fun," one of them enthused as he beelined for Baxter.

Baxter readied his wrench and tapped it threateningly on his palm. "You really want to go, big boy?"

The guard raised his hands to a ready position. "Oh, you have no idea."

Baxter swung the wrench for the guard's shoulder. The Bhoot's hand lashed out so quickly it seemed impossible and clutched at the wrench's end.

Baxter tried to pull it back, but he couldn't move it.

"You puny specters are nothing without your weapons, are you?" the Bhoot jeered. "Ain't it funny that those who treat others like shit in life are rewarded in death. I could kill you over and over again, and I might."

Holding the wrench and fixing Baxter in place, the Bhoot stepped forward and delivered a powerful headbutt.

Baxter stumbled backward, leaving his wrench in the hands of the Bhoot and nearly knocking into those behind him.

"Careful, big guy," Carolyn warned.

Baxter snorted. "Don't tell me, tell him."

Carolyn looked around Baxter at the two Bhoots. "I'd rather not."

But she didn't have a choice. The other Bhoot was engaged in combat with the *Obake*. The Bhoot moved as if he had been pumped full of adrenaline. Defensive blocks were followed by powerful punches, and kicks were all but ignored.

The *Obake* were good fighters, but their blows seemed to bounce off the Bhoots' thick hide, and soon the *Obake* were piled up around the walls, hesitantly staring at the brute.

The guard picked up the final *Obake* by the collar and made to fling her across the room when his eyes widened and the air was pushed out of his lungs.

He took a heavy step backward and stared in disbelief at the slight man standing before him—the wizened Chinese warrior who reserved his words and listened often.

Baxter grinned, then turned his attention back to his own guard. Although he was big, there had to be a way to bring him down. The solution came to him as suddenly as lightning to a conductor.

Baxter reached to his hip and drew his pistol. "Stand down, or I'll put more holes in you than a block of Swiss cheese."

He aimed at the Bhoot and was surprised to see there was no reaction from him. If anything, the Bhoot looked pleased with this latest development.

"That the best you can think of?" the guard taunted.

Baxter gave a one-sided shrug. "Words aren't my thing. You want those, go to Rogue. I'm sure she could fix you up." He steadied the gun and tensed on the trigger.

"Just try me," the Bhoot chuckled.

Using that as his cue, Baxter pulled the trigger. The report was deafening, and he smiled as he imagined the Bhoot collapsing to the ground in pain, moving aside so they could take George and haul ass out of there.

Instead, his face dropped when he saw that the Bhoot was untouched. "Why do you think they use us as heavy artillery cover for their prisoners? We're bulletproof, bitch."

The Bhoot raised his leg and kicked Baxter in the chest.

Baxter flew backward, this time only stopping when he met the door.

Carolyn and Lupe stood open-mouthed, unsure of what to do.

Meanwhile, Porter crawled stealthily along the floor, his eyes locked on the fallen gun.

CHAPTER TWENTY-THREE

<u>Buckingham Palace, London</u>

Jennie was running out of places to search.

She had tried all the usual places the queen frequented—her chambers, several rooms off the second and third-floor landing, most of the east wing—and still there was no sign of her.

Her tiptoeing had turned to a sprint the more desperate she became. All pretense dropped as she ran past faces she had become familiar with, and faces which were new.

The familiar faces wore permanent expressions of fear and upset. The new faces carried guns.

Canute and several of his wraiths followed dutifully along behind Jennie, suggesting places in the palace which she hadn't even known existed. Rooms behind rooms behind rooms. Places Jennie had never had a need to enter in her life, and places which she imagined no one had entered in decades.

She was beginning to wonder if perhaps the queen had abandoned the palace and gone elsewhere when they had a sudden breakthrough.

"Strange time for Her Majesty to be involving herself in such affairs," one pompous specter in a long golden robe whispered to a woman in an ornately embroidered dress. "Is the council *always* in session these days?

"Agreed, these days are strange, but then, these are desperate times." the woman replied. "Never have we fallen under the shadow of such a threat. Without such prompt responses to whistleblowers such as this, we would be living under shadow forever. God bless the queen."

"Still, Her Majesty can't answer the call of every person who knocks on her door."

"Agreed. But what needs be done, be done."

The pompous specter gave a serious nod. "I pray she doesn't work herself too hard. We all know how she can get when she attends to duties beyond her hours."

"Still, they are duties she must attend to."

Jennie didn't even wait until they'd gone out of sight before running past them and toward the council room.

It had been empty when she had passed through. But with a building so large, who was to say they hadn't been circling each other around the corridors, disappearing the moment the other had arrived?

Jennie stood before the large wooden door, intricately carved in a nauseating display of frills, crowns, and ivy. She narrowed her eyes and passed through the door, a strange sense of relief washing over her when she found Victoria sitting on the golden throne.

Jennie walked the red carpet leading to the raised platform, her eyes locked on Victoria.

The queen was oblivious to Jennie's presence, her focus entirely targeted at the two specters standing before her.

"I'm telling you, Your Majesty, we both saw her just moments ago. Strange knockings and workings have been happening at the bottom of the mill. It's the perfect hiding place; think about it."

Victoria looked down her nose at both of them, unimpressed.

Jennie couldn't believe she'd already found two specters to

stand by her side and watch over her. One was a Beefeater she had known as Trent Elskley, and the other was a former heavyweight boxing finalist who unfortunately died of a coronary when he was due to battle for the title. She never caught his name, finding she could not understand a word that came from his mouth. Speaking wasn't his forte; communication usually started and ended with his fists.

"And you say you saw her when?" Victoria pressed.

"Twice yesterday," the other man answered. "Hard to miss with tits like those."

The first specter elbowed him in the side.

"Apologies, Your Majesty. What I meant to say was she was hard to miss with breasts like those. Pop out in that little white blouse, don't they?" He chuckled. "I'm telling ya it was her, all right. Fixed me with a stare under those round sunglasses and made me hot under the collar."

The first specter hit his face with his hand.

Victoria turned to Trent. "This is the big news you had for me? These two idiots believing they saw Rogue a few days ago?"

Trent showed no sign of emotion. "They made a compelling argument."

"Which was?"

"They had information we'd need. You ordered anyone with information to come forward. I believed you'd want to hear them both."

Victoria scowled, massaging her temples with her fingers. "I meant *useful* information. Not two low-breed buffoons who sat on the information for days before reporting it."

"Apologies, Your Grace," the second specter spoke up nervously. "In all fairness, traveling the city is tough at the best of times. It took us some time to find the palace."

Victoria fixed them with an incredulous look, then waved a hand and said in a bored tone, "Very well, thank you for your loyalty to the crown. Guards, show these two specters to the door."

Victoria waited until the pair were ushered out before rising from her throne. "Trent, tell Mr. Clark I'll be awaiting his arrival in the playroom."

Trent nodded, and the pair left. Shortly after, Victoria left the room and made her way down the corridor.

Jennie followed closely behind her, holding her breath. She was within reach, but if she was to be successful, she needed to wait until they were out of reach of prying eyes. The day had broken, which meant that mortals strolled about the corridors, oblivious to the goings-on of the paranormal court.

Victoria, unbothered by anyone who came close, continued with a grim determination, her fingers laced behind her back.

Jennie found it hard to tell even though she knew the truth. *No wonder I was oblivious for so long. The resemblance, the mannerisms—it's uncanny.*

She followed Victoria through a door leading to her chambers. The room was grandiose, most of the space taken up by items of antique furniture topped by squares of lace and curios. The décor made it clear the chamber belonged to royalty in its ornateness and design. Jennie wondered how it was fair that one person could live in such luxury while thousands of mortals slept on the streets every night.

Victoria crossed the room and passed through a portrait on the far side. Jennie followed, striding through a small corridor, then through another wall, where Victoria finally stopped.

Victoria shook her head and looked at a clock on the wall. "If you want a job done right, you do it yourself," she muttered.

"That was exactly my thinking," Jennie agreed, disconnecting from Canute and appearing in the room with Victoria. "Nice place you got here. Can't say I agree with your decoration, though."

Victoria met her eyes, unfazed by her sudden appearance. "I

knew it was only a matter of time before you showed your face. How did you get past my guards?"

"I've got my ways," Jennie told her. She felt the wraiths and was thankful they remained unseen. "You know this is all over, don't you? There's nowhere else to run."

Victoria looked at the ceiling and took a long breath. "You know, for over sixty years, I've been the queen of the paranormal court, something I could never even have dreamed of in my mortal life. I was nothing more than a piece of meat for men to play with, a toy to be used and discarded. On the day I died, I was almost thankful it had happened. The relief was overwhelming."

Jennie moved her hand to the Big Bitch. "You think I give a shit about your whiny little backstory? Save me the pity party. You've twisted everything the court stands for, and all because… what? You wanted power? When I out you as the impostor you are, the world is going to change. Everything is going to be undone."

Victoria stared at her with eyes that weren't her own. "I never went looking for power. Power found me. If you offer water to a man dying of thirst, he'll accept without question. I was given an opportunity, so I took it."

"And killed Victoria in the process."

Victoria smirked. For the first time since Jennie had appeared, there was a victorious smile on her face. "My dear, you really are naïve, aren't you? Do you know what it takes to kill a monarch? Think about what you're saying."

"You're saying Victoria's alive?" Jennie asked.

Victoria chuckled. "I'm not saying anything."

Jennie raised the Big Bitch and trained it at her face. "Who are you?"

Victoria held that irritating smile on her face as she closed her eyes and began to transform. The heavy-bodied monarch with the white headdress vanished before her eyes, leaving behind a beautiful woman with long dark hair and clothes which would be better thrown away than worn.

"Does this help humanize me?" she asked.

Jennie narrowed her eyes. "Who are you?"

The woman wagged her finger, transforming back into Victoria. "Does it really matter?"

"Yes," Jennie stated flatly.

Victoria shrugged. "Well, too bad. We don't all get what we want. You wanted to break into Buckingham Palace and capture the queen, but how are you going to do that in handcuffs?"

She looked over Jennie's shoulder at a man in a black uniform with SIS printed on the chest and back who came into the room and clicked handcuffs around Jennie's wrists.

Jennie latched onto Canute and turned spectral, expecting to slip out of the cuffs and regain her freedom. "What the fuck?" Even as a specter, the handcuffs held, changing form alongside her.

Victoria gave the SIS agent a regal nod. "Not bad."

"Thank you, Ma'am," the agent replied.

"The latest technology," Victoria told Jennie. "Can you believe the advancements that can be made when you pay the right people and focus your resources? Spectral energy-imbued restraints—they're a gamechanger. I'm just happy you're the first criminal we captured with them."

Jennie glared at the impostor, trying to work her hand toward the sword nestled against her hip.

CHAPTER TWENTY-FOUR

<u>Buckingham Palace, London</u>

Baxter focused solely on the big boy in front of him. He had not been involved in many conflicts until he'd met Jennie, but he could hold his own.

Of course, those conflicts had been against specters who viewed his size as a challenge, rather than Bhoots whose size worked very much in his favor.

Staring at the guard, Baxter made a decision. He would fight to the death, and he wouldn't hold back.

He stepped forward and launched a right hook at the Bhoot.

Once again, the Bhoot's hands caught his fist. Baxter went for the left, and the Bhoot grabbed that hand, too.

The guard laughed, setting his feet shoulder width apart as he leaned in and squeezed Baxter's fists. "Dumbass specter, thinking you can take me because you're big."

Baxter saw movement a flurry behind the guard and grinned. "Not quite. I'm just the distraction."

The Bhoot looked down in alarm as Carolyn's foot appeared between his legs and landed heavily in his balls.

The Bhoot's knees pulled together and his hands went to his crotch.

Baxter shook his head and clicked his tongue. "It doesn't matter what type of specter you are, God created the same weakness in every male." With his hands free, he threw another right hook, and this time the blow connected with the Bhoot's jaw. He gave him a left hook, then jabbed him in his nose.

The Bhoot's head flew back, and spectral blood sprayed the air. Baxter pounced on him, taking advantage of the situation, and he and Carolyn rained punch after punch on every part of his body. Some of the *Obake* had recovered enough to get involved in beating the Bhoot until he was unconscious.

Meanwhile, Feng Mian took his stance and beckoned the Bhoot he had knocked over. The Bhoot's face was laced with anger, his attention trained on Feng Mian.

"Son of a bitch," he swore through gritted teeth. "Puny little shit, think you can take on the likes of me—"

Feng Mian struck with the rapidity of a snake. He punched the Bhoot in the stomach, the chest, the throat, and the chin in a rapid flurry of movements.

The Bhoot spluttered and clutched his throat, unsure what the hell had just happened.

Feng Mian held his stance, his face as serene as if he were sowing seeds in the garden.

Riled, the Bhoot dashed forward and threw a giant fist at Feng Mian's head. The force looked set to knock the specter through the wall and out of the room.

But the blow didn't connect.

White light sparked as a shield appeared to block the incoming fist, and the next thing the Bhoot knew was that he'd been blasted back across the room, his giant bulk stopped by hitting the wall.

The *Obake* applauded. Never before had they seen a display of power like this, and they rose to their feet and got involved in the action. With the two Bhoots piled on by specters, it left Baxter, Carolyn, Feng Mian, and a shaken and silent Lupe out of the action.

Baxter looked around the room, hunting. His heart dropped when he spotted Porter on the floor with his fingers millimeters from the pistol.

Carolyn jumped forward and reached in vain for the gun. She was still feet from it. She watched in dismay as Porter's fingers wrapped around the handle, his finger finding the trigger.

She cried out in anguish, but she was determined. She put her every ounce of her energy into wishing she could take the gun. She imagined it in her hand, away from the clutches of the monster, and a strange thing happened.

As Carolyn urged the gun to be hers, a thin tendril of spectral energy snaked away from her hand, growing in thickness as it moved rapidly toward the barrel of the gun.

Porter stood up and brushed himself off, aiming the gun at Baxter's face. He was about to open his mouth to speak when he noticed the tendril and jerked the gun away.

It was too late. The tendril connected with the pistol, and it sprang to Carolyn.

She caught the gun ungracefully and stared at it in amazement.

"Perhaps that is your power," Feng Mian muttered, although his remark was drowned out by Baxter.

"Carolyn, focus!" Baxter yelled. "Neat trick, but we need you in the game."

Carolyn realized what Baxter was saying and held the gun with both hands in front of her, aiming it at Porter. The maneuver didn't feel natural, but then again, Carolyn had never before held a gun.

Well, there's a first time for everything, she thought, eyes flickering from Porter to her hands, which had somehow summoned the weapon.

For the first time in her life, Jennie felt despair creeping in.

She had overcome a thousand obstacles in her career. Had taken on impossible monsters, destroyed life-destroying cults, drug-addled mobsters, even rescued a couple of kittens from trees.

But in all of her years of service, one of the main things which had gotten her through was her ability to outwit the specters. To rely on her gifts and know that, no matter how tough times got, her powers would see her through.

So, what now?

She had transformed from mortal to specter to invisible, and even with the latter, the handcuffs remained fixed firmly around her wrists. The Big Bitch was on the floor and out of reach, and she couldn't quite grasp her sword. She was on her knees with an SIS agent aiming his weapon at her head.

This was an appropriate time to panic.

Who does panic serve? Jennie reminded herself. *Think, Jennie. Nice deep breaths and think.*

The woman disguised as Victoria thanked the agent and knelt before Jennie. She touched her chin and lifted her head to meet her gaze. "I knew I would get you. All these years of fearing the day you would turn, and now I have you. I have to admit, it took a lot longer than I suspected it might, but the most rewarding victories are the ones you have to wait for."

Jennie scowled, unblinking.

The woman smiled for a few seconds, then turned to the agent. "Take her to the cells below and ensure the guards keep her under permanent watch. I'm going to have fun dismantling this human piece by piece."

The agent nodded and dragged Jennie to her feet. He roughly shoved her toward a door Jennie hadn't noticed.

"Just one thing before I go," Jennie called, pausing and turning over her shoulder.

"Yes?" Victoria asked.

"Where is she?" Jennie demanded.

Jennie knew she couldn't say Victoria's name. Why else would the woman have transformed into Victoria again *before* the agent arrived? Even now, at the end of all things, the SIS believed this woman to be the real Victoria, but the question still plagued her mind.

"She's safe," the woman replied. "Doing what she loves best."

Jennie gave a slow nod, then allowed herself to be shoved again by the agent. She stopped when she reached the doorway. "One final, *final* thing."

The woman sighed. "What?"

Jennie frowned. "If I'm heading down to your torture labyrinth, who's going to tell Victoria's family the truth?"

The woman gave Jennie a strange look. "Victoria's... What are you..."

Several balls of black smoke appeared in the room, hovering in the spaces around the woman. She looked up in fear as the smoking balls materialized into wraiths.

The agent drew his pistol, dropping Jennie's arm. He let off several shots but the bullets passed straight through the wraiths and into the wall, leaving small holes behind.

In the distraction, Jennie shuffled her bound hands to one side and thumbed a small pocket she had just for this purpose. She twisted and drew out a vial she deftly fiddled with, ensuring the vial remained upright.

When the lid was off, she leaned backward and tipped the liquid onto her handcuffs, doing everything she could to ensure the acid didn't touch her skin. It chewed through the chain of the cuffs just fine, and soon her hands were free.

Taking advantage of the agent's lack of concentration on his prisoner, Jennie dug her thumb and forefinger into the hollow behind his ear and pressed to send a surge of pain through his nerves and render him unconscious.

The agent crumpled to the floor, where he started to snore gently.

The woman disappeared as the wraiths shrouded her. Jennie gave the agent a swift kick to check that he was truly out of action, then reached down and drew a second set of handcuffs from his pocket. These she used to bind his hands behind his back, ensuring he couldn't get up to any funny business while she addressed the imposter.

Satisfied he wasn't going anywhere, Jennie walked through the smoke and joined the woman in the center of the circle, where the space was as clear as the eye of a hurricane.

Jennie drew the sword and pointed it toward the cowering specter on the floor. "There's a funny thing a lot of people don't know about the royal line. Like, for example, did you know that while the British public believes the bodies of serving monarchs are primarily buried at Westminster Abbey, there's actually a small little graveyard on the western side of London where the bodies are kept?"

The woman was speechless and her eyes darted from wraith to wraith.

Jennie continued, "I discovered the mausoleum some time ago —right around 1936, actually. These guys helped me out on a mission, and I learned a lot about the royal line from them."

The wraiths pulsed with cold anger.

Jennie understood it all too well. "Of course, that was years ago, way before I wised up to what was going on with your little reign of terror. Before you'd gotten involved in the exorcism of your competitors and ensured the line ended with you."

She moved closer and held the tip of the blade to the woman's throat. "I wouldn't have had any clue either if you hadn't have sent me to New York and started all this shit. I suppose I have you to thank for that."

The woman finally found her tongue. "You're crazy. The royal line exorcised themselves to allow for the next monarch to serve. History tells us—"

"Do not believe what is written in history," Jennie told her. "Anyone can weave the story into their own narrative. You of all people should know that."

Jennie addressed the wraiths in turn, pointing at each as she went. Each one she named gave the slightest of nods. "I'd like you to say hi to Henry II, and Williams I and II. That is Harold, and this is Harthacanute."

Jennie paused when she got to Canute. "And this…this is the monarch who began it all—the king who began the paranormal court and brought the order into the history books. I'd like you to say hello to Canute the Dane, also known as Cnut the Great."

Canute loomed over the woman, who shrank beneath his presence.

Jennie chuckled darkly. "Funny thing, really. Considering how vital this guy was to setting up everything you've fought so hard to take over, few remember his name. I guess it really is easy to hide the truth when you sit in the seat of power."

Canute grew in size, his presence becoming a fierce black cloud above them all. "You have tarnished the throne on which our line sits and jeopardized all the court once stood for. Death is too easy a punishment for you."

Jennie drew the sword back.

The woman cowered before Canute. She placed both hands on the floor and muttered incomprehensible words.

"Still, death is the only true punishment," he added.

The woman jerked her head up suddenly, a crazed look in her eyes. The next thing Jennie knew, she had transformed into a perfect clone of Jennie and was staring at the wraiths with hatred in her eyes.

"You've got nothing on me," she hissed. "I will remain the one true quee—"

A blinding flash of light filled the room when Jennie slashed the woman with the saber. The blade made contact, and a deafeningly shrill scream filled the room.

The light vanished as suddenly as it came, leaving a heavy silence behind.

"I never thought *I'd* be the one to kill myself," Jennie quipped as she looked down. There was nothing left of the woman.

Ignoring Jennie's jokes, the wraiths gathered behind her.

"Victoria," Canute asked. "Where is she?"

Jennie holstered her weapon, trying to think it all through logically. She remembered what the woman had told her and gave a resolute nod. "Doing what she loves best."

CHAPTER TWENTY-FIVE

<u>Buckingham Palace, London, 1904</u>

Jennie thanked her guide for leading her through the third floor of the palace, a floor she'd never visited or even thought to explore during her residence here.

The entire floor had been almost deserted, the walls lined with portraits of kings, queens, barons, dukes, and earls. Everywhere she looked, there was a statue, vase, painting, or ornamental decoration. This was where the true hidden beauty of the palace was hidden.

The guide knocked three times on a thick wooden door and waited.

"Come in," a cheery voice called.

The guide pushed the door open for Jennie and introduced her to the room.

Jennie's eyes lit up. The room was a shrine to art. Dotted around the room were easels with paintings in various stages of completion. Brushes were stored in pots on the surfaces, and there were jars of paint in the glass-fronted cabinets around the room.

On the walls were paintings that told stories through their details, pieces that spanned the length and breadth of history. Duplicates and originals spanned the walls from bottom to top, covering the extraordinarily high walls of the room.

Victoria stood in the center, beaming at Jennie with a brush in one hand and paint splattered on her cheeks. "Thank you, Gerald. You may leave us."

The guide bowed low and left them alone.

Jennie tried to take it all in, marveling at each portrait and art piece. She thought about her love for the theater and saw how art could be universal, no matter what medium the artist used.

"It's really something, isn't it?" Victoria remarked, adding a brushstroke to a brightly colored bunch of flowers. "Art is the only universal language—a way to cross language barriers and find a common form of expression. For years, art has been my obsession, but I was unable to practice as I wanted to. I would spend hours—days, even—yearning for time alone to attend to my muse, but the demands of the monarchy are too great. I never got a moment to myself."

Jennie remained quiet, having learned that even with her favorites, the queen was always in a better mood when she was allowed to say her piece.

"Death has granted me few luxuries. I still have many matters to attend to, but now there is time at least to spend a few hours a week here, working on the things that make me happiest."

"I thought ruling made you happy?" Jennie asked, unable to stop herself.

Victoria chuckled and turned to face her fully. "Ruling does make me happy. It's all I ever dreamed it could be, yet ruling in the afterlife is not much different from the way it was in my mortal life. Politicians still argue with each other, the world is still unbalanced, and there are always fires to extinguish." She jabbed her paintbrush at Jennie. "Which is why I summoned you, my little flower."

Jennie bowed dutifully. "Anything you need, Your Majesty."

"You really are my favorite," Victoria told her. "Without you, I'd be left with those tiresome fops who want nothing more than to take the glory without delivering what is needed. You deliver for me every time without fail."

Jennie gave a curt nod. "My purpose is to serve."

"Oh, enough of the formalities." Victoria waved away Jennie's words. "I've called you here because I've got a job for you, and there's a certain level of urgency to the task."

Victoria detailed the job in full while concentrating on her painting. A group of specters calling themselves "The Summoners" were wreaking havoc in the East End and disrupting the public. Several mortals had called attention to the incidents, and now the British Government had contacted the court for assistance.

Jennie memorized every word Victoria said and had already begun working on a plan as she was dismissed and headed toward the door. She paused with her hand on the handle. "Your Majesty?"

"Hmm?"

"Why did you summon me here?" she asked. "This is against our usual process."

"I know your history, King. You're an avid theater-goer, a fan of the arts. I thought it'd help you to view your queen with more fondness if I shared my love of art, too." She moved her hand to the corner of her mouth. "Plus, it's so rare I get a chance to really indulge in my passion. You'll understand I wanted more time here."

"I understand." Jennie nodded respectfully and opened the door.

"Before you go," Victoria called.

Jennie leaned her head back into the room.

Victoria smiled. "Why don't I show you my private collection?"

"Why me?"

Victoria considered this. "Because for some reason I can't quite explain, I trust you."

Buckingham Palace, London

The memory came back to Jennie with crystal clarity as she strode into the east wing of the third floor and retraced her steps of all those years ago.

An entire suite. A private residence built into the palace to allow monarchs to have some privacy. An apartment built into a house built into the palace—that's what this was.

Jennie remembered her excitement when Victoria had led her to these chambers, and the sight as she passed through the doorway still took her breath away a century later.

A live-in gallery was all it could be described as. Jennie couldn't believe it when she saw a familiar face snoozing in an armchair. Clad in a black dress robe and a white headpiece, she hadn't aged.

"Your Majesty?" Jennie called softly.

Victoria started from her slumber, sitting up straight and looking wildly around her. "Porter? Is that you? I told you not to disturb me when I'm…" Her words trailed away when she saw Jennie. "Genevieve? What are you doing here?"

Jennie looked at Victoria incredulously as the wraiths made themselves visible behind her.

Victoria looked at the wraiths and muttered a simple, "Oh, blast!"

Jennie sat with Victoria for a long while with the wraiths standing guard.

Victoria told Jennie everything—how as the years had passed, she had tired of the day-to-day operations of running the paranormal court. There was only so long she could deal with petty politics and scheming. The constant demands were a weight she had to bear.

After ruling the mortal world for sixty-three years and ruling the spectral realm for another fifty or so, she had grown tired and wanted to let someone else take the wheel for a while.

Porter and Yasmine had offered to take over for her, introducing Victoria to the shapeshifting specter. Seeing her opportunity, she took it. "They'd check in with me every few days to ask questions as necessary, and there you have it. Simple, really."

"What have you been doing all these years?" Jennie asked.

Victoria looked around with a crazed expression. "Painting. Resting. Learning. Ruling from afar."

Jennie took the opportunity to explain the turmoil the paranormal kingdom had found itself in. She explained how Porter and Yasmine had abused their power and recruited criminals into the order of the court. She described the fight with the Messino brothers in New York and the civil unrest that had begun to break out across the spectral world.

"The spectral kingdom is on the brink of anarchy," Jennie finished. "No matter what your loyal subjects set out to do with your empire, they've created what could very likely be the next Paranormal War."

Victoria thought about that for a long moment, occasionally glancing at her predecessors, who had remained quiet through the recounting.

When she finally spoke, Jennie wasn't expecting what came out of her mouth.

"Well?" Victoria asked. "What's the problem?"

Jennie stared at her, stunned. "Are you kidding me? Porter and Yasmine and their *Obake* friend have degraded the integrity of the court. They've lied, cheated, and hurt those around them, and now the secret is out. Your Majesty, if stability isn't found soon, there will be an all-out war."

"They've performed exactly as I asked," Victoria replied. "The empire still exists, and I'm still queen. I was the longest-ruling queen in life until my damn great-great-granddaughter took the title. I *will* be the longest-ruling queen in death."

"You're not ruling," Jennie contested quietly. "You're just hiding."

Victoria spun on her. "What do you want from me? Do you know how difficult it is to run an empire? We have specters across the globe demanding my attention at all hours of the day. You try dealing with India, Africa, America, Europe, and every fucking island in the Mediterranean. The Paranormal Empire might be impressive, but it's a lot to maintain."

"Then leave some of it to me." The words left Jennie's mouth before she was aware she was thinking them.

She had never taken the slightest interest in ruling, but after everything she'd seen in the last few weeks, she felt a sudden need to provide stability.

Victoria looked at her as if seeing her for the first time. "Excuse me?"

This time Jennie said it with conviction. "Leave some of it to me. You said it yourself— the volume of problems is cumbersome. I'll take some of the load."

Victoria scoffed. "*You?*"

"Why not?" Jennie shrugged. "I've served by your side for over a hundred years. I've seen every layer of the paranormal court, and I know it like the back of my hand."

Victoria stammered. "I couldn't... You can't possibly be serious?"

"I've never been more serious about anything in my life." Now that Jennie thought about it, the words rolled off her tongue. She grew excited at the prospect. "America is in the worst state of turmoil. Following New York, turf wars are springing up all over the country. That place is touchy at the best of times. How's it going to be after this?"

Victoria nodded.

"They were the last ones you were trying to reign in." Jennie continued. "Efforts aren't going well. I will do you a solid and leave this country in order to restore peace overseas."

"Why would I let you do that?" Victoria asked. "According to Porter, we were making progress. We had established connections with the government and assisting in dealing with some of their longer-standing issues."

Jennie met Victoria with a determined stare. "You're not going to let me. I'm going to take it."

A pregnant pause passed between them.

"I'm sorry," the queen enunciated in a low voice. "Did I mishear you?"

Jennie shook her head. "You did not. The way I see it, there's only one option here. I am under no obligation to serve you, the country, or the paranormal court anymore. I'm beyond disappointed that I looked up to you, and you turned out to be a coward. You, on the other hand… Well, you have thousands of faithful specters who still believe in you and don't know the truth behind everything that has transpired. I'll leave your piss-poor excuse for a domain and show the world what justice truly looks like. You will leave me alone, and I won't hear so much as a peep from your court unless I call for backup. You got that?"

Jennie extended a hand toward Victoria, who appeared incredulous at the offer. Her face moved through a kaleidoscope of emotions, from entertained to concerned to confused before she frowned and gritted her teeth. "You're blackmailing the queen of England? In front of her kin?"

Jennie gave a half-shrug. "You've disgraced the country and your empire in front of them. Whose side do you think they're on right now?"

Victoria stared at Canute for a long moment before sighing and taking Jennie's hand. "You had better know what you're doing out there," she warned.

"I never know what I'm doing," Jennie replied, walking away. "I work it out along the way."

EPILOGUE

<u>London</u>

Shortly after Jennie left Buckingham Palace, a public order was issued by the real Queen Victoria, ending the search for Rogue across London.

Porter Sykes was demoted to the lower levels of the paranormal court and spent his time formulating plans to regain his high station, although that was likely never going to happen.

After the real queen returned to her throne, she found her passion rekindled enough to warrant identifying a new set of obedient lapdogs who hadn't threatened her entire order and failed to keep the whole damn thing secret.

Upon leaving Buckingham Palace, Jennie found her comrades in the cells below the palace and brought George back to her place beneath the Savoy theater. There they remained for several days, celebrating their victory and discussing Jennie's plans for America, each specter completely behind the idea of bringing a new order into being.

"That's a tall order," Baxter exclaimed, laughing one night as they drew plans on a large sheet of paper in the center of Jennie's living room. "You've seen what the US is capable of, and that was just on a tiny island. Imagine what it'll be like on the West Coast or in the South."

"Every great idea starts somewhere," Jennie told him with a broad grin on her face. She held a mimosa in each hand, and there were a few empty glasses on the table in front of her. "All we've got to do is find a way to execute and bring peace to our transatlantic spectral cousins."

"But won't starting a new order get us to the same endpoint as the paranormal court?" Carolyn asked, sitting so close to Feng Mian that he looked uncomfortable. "We'll end up right where we are now."

George shook his head emphatically. His bruises were starting to heal, and only a thin line remained where Porter had cut him. "This is Rogue we're talking about."

Jennie raised one of her drinks. "I've told you, George. My friends call me Jenny."

George chuckled, a playful look in his eye. "Since when did the great and powerful Rogue have friends?"

Jennie blushed, wondering how she had spent so much of her life alone when being surrounded by people who cared about her was like this.

"It'll be different because the heart of the organization will be about building peace among specters," Jennie told Carolyn. "It won't be mandatory to join, but we will be there for mortals and specters alike. We will fight for specters to have the right to choose how they live their lives, and we will become the reigning independent union that unites everyone and restores peace. We'll be everything the queen's court should have been. Everything it once was."

Baxter looked at Jennie with eager eyes.

"What?" Jennie said uncertainly. "What are you thinking?"

Baxter grinned. "I've got the perfect name for it. Your real name is Genevieve King, right?"

They all waited expectantly.

"The King's Court!"

Jennie rolled her eyes and laughed. "We'll see."